The Hillside Roble

In This Series

DAGMARMIURA.COM

The Hillside Roble

The Hillside Roble

George Bixley

Published by Dagmar Miura
Los Angeles
www.dagmarmiura.com

The Hillside Roble

First published 2018

ISBN: 978-1-942267-70-6

"You eat like a freaking horse," Slater said, watching Andy devour a stack of pancakes. They were having breakfast at a greasy diner behind the train station. It always made Slater a little nervous to be in here, as the joint was close to the county jail, and it was open all night, so it was usually crawling with cops. But Andy had wanted pancakes.

"I have a high metabolism," Andy said, setting down his fork. It was true; his random twitching meant his muscles did twice as much work as Slater's. "CP is the best diet ever. Those Westside women with their stomach bands and their collagen injections and their anal bleaching would be completely jealous if they knew … how much I can eat and yet still see my abs."

Slater scoffed at that and slurped at his coffee. He'd been sleeping over at Andy's a few nights a week since they'd met, and they had a lot of fun, although Slater had made it clear he didn't need a damn boyfriend. Besides the sex, Andy was useful to have around, as he had a knack for digging up stuff about people online that otherwise remained hidden.

The busboy cleared their plates, and said something to Slater in Spanish.

"*Gracias,*" Slater said, and Andy grinned as the guy walked away.

"You have no clue … what he said, do you."

"None," Slater said, and chuckled. It happened a lot—he had his father's thick black hair and Latin American coloring, and half the people in Los Angeles were Hispanic.

"I'm amazed it doesn't piss you off," Andy said.

"Why would it?"

"It doesn't take much to … piss you off."

Slater shot him a look and went to pay at the register, eyeing a table of deputies involved in conversation over their morning coffee, and waited as Andy worked his arms into the sleeves of his crutches and ambled toward the door.

Slater's classic Thunderbird was parked right outside, sleek and black in the early light, and they rode in amicable silence the few blocks into downtown LA, back to Andy's loft on Broadway.

Slater waited while Andy maneuvered his way out of the car and onto the curb—he knew better by now than to offer to help. On the surface it looked precarious, even aimless sometimes, but eventually Andy achieved what he was trying to do. Once he'd pushed the door closed, Slater pulled back into the traffic.

His periodic employer in the insurance business had called him in, which was very good news—Slater needed to work. Cudahy Mutual's offices were nearby, in an office tower in the Financial District, and he headed there, waiting to turn left through the crosswalk for the throng of pedestrians in their office drag. As he approached the ramp down into the parking garage, a street space opened up in front of him, and he nosed the Thunderbird into it.

After he fed the meter, he took his satchel out of the trunk and slung it over his shoulder, then navigated the crowded sidewalk toward the office building's lobby. From behind him something slammed into his shoulder, not quite hard enough to make him stumble. As he turned to look, a guy on a powered scooter, wearing jeans and a T-shirt, maybe still a teenager, lost his balance from the collision, then stepped off and scooped up his wheels, ignoring Slater and striding away. Slater hustled to catch up to him, and when he was right behind the guy, hooked his boot in front of his ankle and shoved the middle of his back. He tumbled to the pavement, his scooter clattering on the concrete, and rolled onto his butt, looking up at Slater, his eyes wide.

"Watch where you're going," Slater said, and stepped past him, into the lobby of the office tower and up the elevator to the thirty-fourth floor.

The receptionist, her blond hair swept into an updo, scowled when she looked up and saw him walking in.

"Hello, Crystal," Slater said, standing in front of her desk. The fact that he remembered her name didn't seem to impress her, so he dug deep, way back into his childhood, to recall the techniques a shrink had once tried to teach him about relating to people. Feigning civility, he said, "I believe Della is expecting me."

Wordlessly she picked up the phone. "Mr. Ibáñez to see you."

Slater put his hands on his hips, watching her, unable to maintain the charade. Even though he was expected, as Della had summoned him, he still had to stand here, waiting through the pointless process like a chump.

"Go on back," Crystal said finally, replacing the receiver.

"Thank you," Slater said intently, glaring at her and raising his voice.

Della's office door was open, and he knocked

on it as he entered, admiring the view out her windows of the hazy city stretching to the horizon. Today Della was wearing a low-cut blue dress, cinched at the waist, her hair sprayed into a stylish helmet. In her late fifties, she was still shapely.

"Hey, hot stuff," she said, leaning back in her chair.

"I wasn't sure I was going to get past your guard dog."

Della grinned. "Crystal is good at her job."

"Despite the attitude," Slater said flatly, dropping into the chair in front of her desk. "So what have you got for me?"

"I need you to look into a claim. A painting went missing from an art gallery, and it looks like Cudahy Mutual is on the hook."

"How did it go missing?"

"It disappeared during a party—a reception, they said—in front of a room full of people. No one saw it happen."

Slater frowned. "They don't have security cameras?"

"There was a power failure. It took out the cameras for forty minutes."

"This happened after dark?"

"Right."

"So either someone took advantage of the lights going out, or it was planned for cover during the theft."

"Plus it was a party, so there are dozens of potential suspects." She opened a file on her desk and riffled through it, handing a sheet across to him.

It was a printout of a painting, and Slater studied the image. A towering, sprawling oak tree stood alone on a grassy slope, stark against the deep-blue sky. The muted dark-green leaves and the yellowed grass implied it was late summer or fall, before the winter rains, the same season they were in now, with the days growing short but still hot and dry. He couldn't see the brushstrokes in this printout, but he could tell it was a detailed and realistic rendering of a rural scene.

"It's old," Della said, "like nineteenth century. It's called the *Hillside Roble*."

Slater would have called it a valley oak, but maybe back then people used the Spanish name. Lots of California place-names used Spanish words, so even people like Della, with no under-standing of the language, knew it was pronounced *roh-blay*. The signature was visible in the bottom corner, "Jos. Nelson."

"I've never heard of the artist," Slater said.

"Neither have I."

"How big is it?"

"Eighteen by twenty-two, and it's insured for ten million. We'll probably pay out less than that. It changed hands about a year ago, when the gallery bought it for six million."

"Seriously?" Slater demanded, meeting her gaze. "Why so much? It's a painting of a tree."

She shrugged. "Value in art isn't about the art; it's about trends. The latest California gold rush is the tech industry. Those people have obscene amounts of money. They think they own the place, and that painting is archetypal California."

"That it is," Slater said, studying the image again. "I've seen a dozen places like this along the 101. Who's the claimant?"

"The gallery—E. L. Hardin Fine Art. The address is in the paperwork." She slid the rest of the file toward him.

"What do you need me to find out?" Slater asked, shuffling the printout into the folder.

"Ideally, I'd like to find the painting," she said, and grinned. "Failing that, maybe you can find out who took it."

Slater nodded. "Anything hinky in the claim?"

"Nothing that jumps out. I called you in on this because of the dollar value."

Slater stood up, flipping open his satchel and sliding the folder inside. "I'll see what I can do."

Della rose and stepped around her desk as Slater moved to the door. "So how's your love life?"

Slater frowned. "Extremely guy-centric."

"Well, if it gets boring, there's plenty happening on the other side of the street."

"That's never going to happen, sister."

Della laughed. "It never hurts to try."

"And you always do," Slater said, then headed back to the elevator lobby.

Walking past the receptionist's desk, Slater held up a palm and said, "Bye, Crystal," but she just frowned, studiously ignoring him. Slater sighed. Some people just didn't have very good social skills.

It was a short drive to his office, in the Fashion District, and he parked in the surface lot across the street, waving to the parking attendant as he left. They never checked that he had his pass, as they recognized the distinctive Thunderbird.

Once an office building, the 1920s high-rise now hosted myriad small clothing factories, and Slater stepped through the throng of day laborers hanging around the entrance, waiting for gigs sewing or cutting or transporting garments. It was a clean industry, at least, although the elevators and the hallways were years overdue for renovation, the linoleum torn and blackened from decades of feet treading on it, and during business hours the building hummed with the sound of sewing machines.

Up on the ninth floor, the offices he shared with his business partner, Max, were around behind the elevator shaft. As he went in, Slater admired the lettering on the door. All this was still pretty new:

SLATER IBÁÑEZ
MAXIMILLIAN CONROY
INVESTIGATIONS

They had three small rooms—an office for each of them behind a cramped reception space that held an unoccupied desk and a coat rack. Max was in, sitting at his desk, and Slater stood in his doorway.

"You picked up an insurance gig?" Max asked, leaning back in his chair, the butt of his weapon visible in its holster under his dark suit jacket. Thick-set and ruddy, Max was a great guy to partner up with, as he had a PI license and could do things that Slater couldn't. Slater regularly wanted to punch him in the face, but as long as he suppressed that instinct, they worked pretty well together.

Slater patted his satchel. "I'm kind of relieved to be working again."

"I'm there too, brother—I got hired last night to do a window-shade case."

"Cheating wife, or cheating husband?" Slater asked. He didn't envy Max the window-shade jobs, with all the sneaking around and the emotionally unhinged targets, but there were a lot of them, and they paid the bills.

"The guy thinks his fiancée is cheating on him. Lucky for me she works in the fashion biz, so most of the day she's within two blocks of here."

Slater went into his own little office, setting his satchel on his desk. He pulled out the case file Della had given him and then got comfortable in his chair, swinging his boots up on his desk, and started going through it. The claim paperwork seemed straightforward, despite the absurd dollar value on the missing painting. E. L. Hardin was actually the owner, he saw, not just an ancestor or a made-up name. The *E* stood for Elijah, and there was no photo of the guy, but a printout of a newspaper article about the gallery's opening a couple of years ago explained that he had spent "many years working in the entertainment industry." Photos accompanying the article showed a renovated industrial space, stark white walls under a high arching ceiling with exposed wooden beams.

The place would be open now, so he packed up the file and slung on his satchel, waving to Max as he left.

TWO

The gallery was nearby, in the Arts District, just a few minutes' drive. A century ago this neighborhood had been factories and warehouses for the growing metropolis, then artists had taken over the roomy spaces when industry had moved to larger quarters. Today artists couldn't afford to live among the tony galleries and trendy restaurants, their studios displaced by lofts for high-income residents with nothing to invest in the neighborhood but cash, which paradoxically sterilized the place, killing the bohemian vibe they'd moved here for.

Slater found the gallery on a quiet side street, and cruised past, parking the Thunderbird farther up the block. As he walked back to it, he saw that the building had two storefront businesses at one end, and the gallery at the other. In front of one of the shops, a dozen or more powered foot scooters, rentable by smart phone and so beloved of creative types, were jumbled together in a pile that spilled into the gutter.

More interesting were the carob trees planted in front of the gallery. They'd been properly limbed up, so the branches were high, out of the way of passing pedestrians. He had to admit it was a good choice for a street tree—they looked elegant and didn't hog up water.

The front of the gallery was styled as a retail space, with tall windows and a glass door. Pulling it open, he stepped inside, finding the cavernous room quiet and devoid of life. A desk just inside on the left was deserted, without even a chair, and a banner painted on the opposite wall in tall rust-orange letters announced CALIFORNIA LANDSCAPES. The artworks, mounted at eye level on the plain white walls, were indeed landscapes, old-school oil paintings like the *Hillside Roble*: pine trees and mountains, yuccas speckling the Mojave, that skinny waterfall in Big Sur. At the back of the yawning space, metal stairs led up to a wide catwalk and two office doors, each with an adjacent window looking down on the gallery. Those would have been the white-collar offices when this place had been a factory, and they probably still served as the boss's perch.

From a doorway under the stairs, a woman appeared, pushing herself in a wheelchair. It was a sporty model, not the medical version, moving remarkably fast across the polished concrete toward him. Her sleeveless top revealed the musculature of her arms, and the short blond hair might even be natural, he thought, as there were no dark roots. Her paleness was made more dramatic by bright-red lipstick, and she was model-thin, probably a prerequisite in a trendy industry like shilling art.

"Can I help you?" she asked, pulling up and subtly giving Slater the once-over.

Dark-skinned and wearing denim, Slater knew that he didn't look like someone seeking to spend big on oil paintings. He told her his name, and said, "I'm looking into the theft of the *Hillside Roble* for Cudahy Mutual."

The woman sighed, not hiding her annoyance, and turned away, rolling around behind the glass-topped desk. "I did an extensive interview about all that with the police detective."

"As boring as it might be for you," Slater said intently, "you're going to have to talk to me too. What's your name?"

"I'm Birgit."

"You work the front desk?"

"Reception and sales," she said, meeting his gaze.

"Were you here when the painting disappeared?"

"It was the opening of the exhibition," she said, frowning. "I was here, but I didn't see anything."

Slater studied her for a moment. "Where was the painting being displayed that night?"

Birgit swiveled her wheels and coasted toward the back of the vast gallery space, stopping in front of the wall at the bottom of the stairs. It wasn't visible from the front desk, but as Slater approached, he saw there were two hooks mounted close together on a bare stretch of wall. The card below the empty space read HILLSIDE ROBLE. The void left by the missing piece was emphasized by the works still hanging on either side—on the left was a painting of a stand of sequoias, its brushwork slightly impressionistic, titled REDWOODS on the card below. On the other side was a photorealistic rendering of a rocky headland labeled LOS OSOS. Leaning closer, Slater saw that it was an oil too. One of them had a round red dot stuck on the wall beside the title card, and the other didn't.

"The red dot means it's sold?" Slater asked.

Birgit nodded. "Standard gallery practice."

"Why didn't you put something else in that spot?" he said, gesturing to the empty space.

"Displaying the hangers emphasizes the loss. Clearly something's missing."

Slater looked around the room. "All these are nineteenth-century works?"

"Mostly early twentieth century. The theme of the exhibition is California landscapes."

"Yeah, I can read," Slater muttered, and walked toward the back wall.

The gallery's rear door, similar to the one at the front, was heavy glass. It was propped open, and Slater could see it led into a hallway. Adjacent to it, under the overhead catwalk, was a door marked PRIVATE.

"What's in here?" he asked.

"The workroom."

Slater pushed open the door, which didn't have a lock, and flipped on the light. The windowless space had a low ceiling and a broad worktable in the middle. Framed canvases and folded cardboard boxes were stacked against one wall. A wire shelving unit at the back held tools, containers, and other clutter.

Stepping back into the gallery, Slater asked, "Are any of the other paintings worth ten million dollars?"

Birgit scoffed. "Not even close. All of these are just filler to support the main piece."

"The *Hillside Roble*."

"Correct. None of the others would break ten grand retail."

Slater gestured to the painting beside the

empty hooks. "How much for the sequoias?"

"They're redwoods. I think that one is twenty-eight fifty."

"How many people were here for the opening?"

Birgit sighed. "Maybe sixty? The bar was set up over there, beside the front desk. The security guard was hanging out near the door."

"What guard?" Slater asked, frowning. Why hadn't there been any mention of a guard in the paperwork?

"I have his name," she said, and rolled back to her desk. Slater followed, taking in the space. It was a big gallery, the ceiling twenty feet overhead, with a lot of floor space; it wouldn't have been all that crowded with sixty people in here.

Peering at her computer screen, Birgit said, "The guy's name was Rogelio. Burly dude with a black mustache. He works for Montclair Security." She read a phone number, and Slater pulled out his phone to thumb-type it into a note.

"Tell me what happened when the power failed," he said, looking at her again.

"The lights went out, and the emergency lights came on in the corners, so it wasn't pitch black. Just dim." She pointed to the fixtures, each essentially a pair of spotlights with a bulky battery, mounted high on the wall. One was behind her desk, the other in the back corner near the stairs and the empty hooks. Next to each of the devices was a subtle security camera, aimed down at the gallery space.

"The streetlights were still on," Birgit continued, "so I knew it wasn't an outage in the whole neighborhood. People weren't panicking, but they did start moving onto the street."

"What's out the back way?"

"Go see for yourself," she said.

Slater walked back under the catwalk and through the propped-open door. The hallway led straight back and had two other doors in it, both heavy and secure, with deadbolt locks. These were the other businesses in the building, Slater realized. One had a chirpy green logo of a swirling bird painted on it, and the other was labeled THOUGHTFUL DISRUPTION. That sounded like a libertarian tech company, which definitely fit with the trash pile of rental scooters out front.

At the far end, the outer fire door was also propped open. Slater stuck his head out, finding a gritty alley lined by high fences but wide enough to accommodate a couple of parking spaces, neither of them in use now. Back inside, opposite the offices, a door labeled EQUIPMENT ROOM bore a jagged graphic of a lightning bolt inside a black triangle, along with the admonishment DO NOT BLOCK DOOR.

Slater tried the handle, and finding it unlocked, pushed it open. A half flight of steps led down to an unfinished concrete floor. Pulling it closed again, he walked back up the hallway to the gallery. A security camera was mounted above the gallery's back entrance, he saw, aimed at the hall. That made three, counting the two he'd seen inside.

"Those look like the back doors of other businesses," he called to Birgit as he approached her desk. "I thought E. L. Hardin owned the building."

"He does, but he rents those two units to tech-industry people."

"Was the door to the alley open during the party?"

"It was," she said, jutting out her chin and meeting his eye. "It was hot in here."

Slater put his hands on his hips. "When the lights went out, where was the guard, Rogelio?"

"I wasn't watching him. It was dark for maybe five minutes before someone said 'Where's the *Hillside Roble*?' Eli started shouting 'Nobody leaves,' and Pilar tried to block the front door."

"Who's Pilar?"

"The gallery manager," Birgit said, absently adjusting her wheels and pivoting her chair. "She should actually be here by now."

"She locked the front door?"

"She was shouting 'Don't leave,' but you can't hold people hostage. It was too late anyway—lots of them had already left."

"What happened then?"

"Screaming, and accusations, and freaking out. Pilar called the cops, but the utility company got here first."

"The DWP?"

"I guess that's who it was. The truck was in the alley—I saw the yellow flashing lights. The power came back on fast. They only worked on it for a few minutes. They were gone again when the cops got here."

Slater watched her, thinking it through. "So during the blackout, did you notice anyone go missing?"

Birgit gestured helplessly. "There were so many people, and I didn't know most of them. I was working the desk, bugging anyone who came by to sign the mailing list. I was supposed to handle sales, even though there weren't any."

"What about E. L Hardin, and Pilar? Where were they?"

"Pilar was running things. She was in and out, upstairs and into the alley, and managing the bartender and the security guard. Eli was just standing around schmoozing, not really working, so he didn't go anywhere."

"What happened when the police got here?"

"Most of the guests were gone. A cop in uniform interviewed Eli, then Pilar, and then me, and the others searched the gallery, top to bottom. They didn't find the *Hillside Roble*."

"Who do you think took it?" Slater said, watching her closely.

"I have no idea," she said, and looked toward the front door as it swung open.

The woman coming in was curvy, with long black hair, wearing a beige skirt with a bulky dark bag over one shoulder. Pushing her sunglasses up on her head, her eyes narrowed when she caught sight of Slater.

"This is Pilar," Birgit said. "This guy is from the insurance company."

Slater dug in his pants pocket for his business card and handed it to her.

Studying it, Pilar said, "Ibáñez," pronouncing it the Spanish way, then said something in Spanish. The only word Slater could parse was *español*.

"Sorry," he said. *"No comprendo."*

"What are you doing for the insurance company?" she asked, her eyes flicking over him.

"Research," Slater said flatly. "Where were you when the lights went out?"

Pilar pulled off her sunglasses and dropped them into her bag, which she set on the end of Birgit's desk.

"At that specific moment I was standing by the bar," she said, meeting his gaze. "People started to leave, and they were loud, laughing it up, probably because of the booze. After a few minutes someone started yelling about the *Hillside Roble*. I went over to look, and sure enough, it was gone."

"Where was Hardin?"

"I don't know. He was here when we noticed the painting was missing, because he's the one who was screaming loudest."

"What about Birgit—where was she?"

"I'm not sure," Pilar said, not looking at her. "Maybe here at the desk?"

"You leave me out of it," Birgit said hotly. "I didn't steal anything."

Slater eyed her, then asked Pilar, "Did anything odd happen during the power failure?"

She frowned. "Yeah—the *Hillside Roble* disappeared."

"How is it possible, in a room full of people, that no one saw anything?"

Pilar stepped around him, toward the back of the gallery. "Take a look at where the emergency lights are."

Slater followed, standing beside her and gazing up at the dual spotlights.

"The gallery was dark, and those were the only lights. If you looked into that corner, you just saw glare. The painting isn't very big, and if someone was standing there, no one would have seen them carry it out the back."

"Why was it hung there, specifically? It's

kind of out of the way, considering it's the most important artwork."

"You don't put the best stuff in view of the front door," Pilar said, folding her arms. "People have to come in and look around before they get to it."

"I need to see video of the party up to the power failure," Slater said.

"No way," Pilar said, shaking her head. "I already made copies for the police."

"If you choose not to produce it, I'll happily spike your insurance claim today," Slater said, raising his voice. Of course he didn't have that power, but he knew the threat alone would be a motivator.

Pilar glared at him for a moment, then sighed. "We can look at it in my office."

She grabbed her bag from Birgit's desk and then strode across to the metal stairs, trotting up. Slater followed, glancing at the empty hooks flanked by the sequoias and rocky Los Osos. The stairs had been repainted in bright blue, but they looked antique, probably dating to when the building had been an industrial space. He waited on the catwalk, gazing down at the gallery, while Pilar unlocked one of the offices. It was a small room, the only window the one looking across the catwalk into the gallery, and it contained little more than a desk and a pair of file cabinets.

Pilar sat at her desk and shook the mouse to wake her computer. Slater stood watching; there was no other chair. Lifting the blotter, she glanced at a sticky note underneath before dropping it again and typing on her keyboard. A password, Slater realized. She had it written down on her desktop, and she'd let him see where it was.

"Here," she said, gesturing to the screen.

Slater stepped around beside her to see a list of files, each with a date and time. She clicked on a calendar in the corner, which brought up a different list.

"The cameras are cloud-based," she said, looking up at him. "From the start of the party, there's over an hour of footage from two different cameras, plus the one pointed at the back hallway. You really want to watch them all?"

"I do," he said. "Can I use your chair?"

Pilar frowned in annoyance but rose, letting him sit down.

"Show me Hardin," Slater said, and Pilar stooped to use the mouse, clicking one of the files and then fast-forwarding through the video. It was a view of the gallery from behind Birgit's desk, distorted by the wide-angle lens and not high-resolution. Maybe two dozen people were standing around, some studying the paintings on the wall, but most clustered around the bar.

"That's him," Pilar said, pointing at a figure on the screen.

The guy was tall and dark-skinned, and it was hard to tell from the grainy image, but he seemed to be bald. Slater couldn't get a sense of his facial features, but he looked buff—definitely fuckable.

"The video ends right when the lights went out?" Slater asked, looking up at her.

"It cuts out a little before that. The cameras upload in ten-minute chunks, so some of it got lost. Without power, they didn't record anything for about forty minutes."

Looking back to the screen, Slater asked, "Do you know everyone in the room?"

"I don't know any of them," she said. "We had a list of people that we invited, but it was an open-door event. With all the bars and restaurants, there's lots of foot traffic in this neighborhood."

Slater fast-forwarded through the file, then clicked on the next one in the list, pointing to a guy in a black jacket who had strayed into view. "Is that the security guard?"

Pilar leaned closer, peering at the screen. "I think so. He stayed by the door the whole time."

"Why was there only one person working security?" Slater asked, watching her. "If I had a ten-million-dollar painting, I'd have eyes on it."

"That was Eli's call. There was a guard here, but he missed the theft."

"Who do you think took the painting?"

"No clue," she said, shrugging.

"How did they take it out? Through the front door, or into the alley?"

"How would I know that?" she said, raising her voice.

"OK, Pilar—settle down." He watched her for a moment. "When did the party start?"

Pilar sighed impatiently. "People started arriving around eight. Eli introduced the painting around nine."

Turning back to the screen, Slater found the file with the time stamp at nine o'clock and clicked on it, fast-forwarding to the point where Eli stood near the metal stairs, beside the *Hillside Roble*, addressing the crowd. The painting itself was just a few green pixels in a smear of yellow and blue, distorted by the camera angle, but it was there, hanging where the empty hooks were today.

"Thank you all for being here," Eli said, his voice deep and clear, gesturing with the plastic cup in his hand. "I hope most of you have had a chance to see the star of the evening, Joseph Nelson's *Hillside Roble*. Nelson wasn't well-paid in his lifetime, and he died impoverished and in obscurity, probably of consumption, like any self-respecting great artist." The crowd tittered, and Eli smiled, waving his glass. "But today his work is considered the best of California."

Slater hit fast-forward; he didn't need to hear that. Eli spoke for a few more minutes, and the crowd started to dissipate as the video ended. Slater pulled up the next video, watching intently. In his peripheral vision Pilar hovered, shifting her weight from one foot to the other. Eventually she turned to the window and pulled up the venetian blinds, then opened her office door, propping it wide with a doorstop.

"I'll be downstairs," she said, and Slater grunted in acknowledgment, not taking his eyes off the screen.

As soon as he heard her footfalls on the stairs, he pulled out his phone and lifted the blotter on the desktop. Making sure the flash was off, he photographed the sticky note Pilar had glanced at, then made sure the writing was legible in the image. It was a short string of letters and numbers—definitely a password.

Sliding his phone back into his jeans, he watched several more of the video files in fast mode, from the front camera and from the one at the back of the gallery. Lots of people stepped up to examine the *Hillside Roble*, but no one dared to touch it, and no one spent more than a minute or two with it. The gap in the video files was closer to an hour, even though Pilar had said it was forty minutes. The last file before the blackout wasn't insightful, although the room was more crowded than it had been earlier, when Eli had made his speech. After the blackout the room was almost empty, the *Hillside Roble* missing from its spot on the wall. From the other camera's viewpoint, the bartender was cleaning up, and a couple of cops were standing in front of Birgit's desk, asking her the same kinds of questions Slater had. He listened to her answers, but nothing she said contradicted what she and Pilar had told him today.

Files from the camera aimed at the back hallway confirmed what Birgit had said, that the door to the alley had been propped open that night. How naive could these people be? It's almost like they were asking to get jacked. In one video, sometime before Hardin's speech, Pilar, clad in a dark-red dress, walked out to the alley and then back in again. Later a couple of party guests strolled out, drink cups in hand.

Overall, the videos backed up Birgit's assertion that she was at the front desk the whole time. Pilar wasn't always in view, but she spent a lot of time around the bar. The bartender never strayed from his post, and the security guard was only visible occasionally in the doorway, rarely stepping inside. Eli Hardin walked out twice, and went up the stairs once, disappearing for a few minutes, but as Birgit had said, mostly he was just chatting with his guests. Still, in the time after the end of the video coverage, and in the semidarkness, any of these people could have pilfered the painting and walked out to the alley unnoticed.

Slater sighed and stood up, arching his back. He could look at this stuff again at his leisure, now that he had Pilar's password. As he walked down the stairs, he saw that Birgit was parked at one side of the gallery, explaining a painting to a woman in white pants, her expensive-looking hair cascading down her back.

"You can see that the artist had an aesthetic sense that stretched well beyond his lifetime," Birgit was saying. "The focus is on his psychological interaction with the landscape. Are we part of it, or are we mere observers? Where does one draw the line between objectivity and the experiential? A sophisticated observer can see that transcendence in the sheer luminosity of the brushstrokes."

Slater grinned at that and walked to the front desk, where Pilar was absorbed in the computer screen.

"Show me the invite list for the opening," he said.

She looked up at him, furrowing her brow. "I gave it to the police."

Slater frowned. "You didn't keep a copy?"

"Eli might have one. I don't."

"Where is Eli Hardin, anyway?"

"He doesn't come in every day."

"Give me his cell number, then."

"I can't do that. He's a very private person."

He called to Birgit, loud enough to interrupt her conversation. "What's Eli's cell number?"

Birgit scowled at him. "No way, brother," she said, and turned back to her client.

"We'll have him call you," Pilar said.

"If you're giving me the runaround," Slater snapped, "I'll make you regret it."

"Dude, chill," she said, raising her voice. "I'll tell him it's important."

"Give me the name of the cop assigned to the case. Unless he's a delicate shy type person too?"

"Detective Torres," Pilar said. "I have her card at my desk."

"I have a copy in my top drawer," Birgit called, wheeling toward them. Her customer was on her own now, strolling along the wall and studying the landscapes.

Pilar stepped back to let Birgit open her drawer, and she handed the card to Slater. He set it on the desktop and snapped a photo of it.

"Do you two have business cards?" he asked, eyeing them in turn.

Birgit plucked the detective's card from the desktop and exchanged it for two others in her drawer. "One for each of us," she said, handing them to Slater.

Scanning them briefly, he saw that they both

listed surnames and email addresses. Sliding them into his hip pocket, he glared at Pilar. "Hardin had better call me," he said, and walked out to the street.

THREE

On the way to his car, he thought about the gallery. Anyone in the city could have wandered in the back door when the lights went out and lifted the *Hillside Roble* off the wall. It would be easy to report to Della right now that the gallery had failed completely to take appropriate security measures, which would mean she could void the insurance claim. But there might be more to it, and he wanted to talk to the owner, Eli Hardin. Besides, if he bailed out now, he'd only get paid for a day's work.

Climbing into the Thunderbird, he checked the rearview mirror and then looked at his phone, searching the web for the phone number Birgit had given him for the security company. It was legit, it seemed, as the number was connected to a business called Montclair Security. Slater dialed, surprised that a human being answered the phone. He explained who he was, and that he wanted to talk to Rogelio. It must be a small office, he realized, as the woman knew exactly what he was talking about.

"Rogelio is on a construction site in South Park," she said. "They work until six. You could talk to him there."

South Park was near his office, and he twisted the key in the ignition, pulling onto the street and heading that way.

The address she'd given him was a towering concrete shell with a construction crane perched on top—another in a sporadic series of residential towers built with mainland Chinese capital in the sterile neighborhood. Parking along the construction fence, he climbed out and looked up. If they kept building these things, this town was going to look like Manhattan.

Walking up on the gate into the site, he spotted Rogelio right away. The guy was thick, and had slicked-back jet-black hair and a little mustache. A shiny badge was pinned to his dark jacket, giving him the air of authority, if not really any legal right to it.

"Rogelio?" Slater greeted him as he approached.

He frowned, a worried look in his eye.

"Yeah—who's asking?" He was a native speaker, Slater realized, his accent from a blue-collar neighborhood.

"I work for an insurance company," Slater said. "I wanted to ask you about working at the Hardin Gallery."

Rogelio shoved his hands into his jacket pockets and stepped back against the construction fence. "I didn't see anything," he said.

"From the video, it looked like you were on the sidewalk most of the time."

"All of the time," he said emphatically.

"I know what it's like to work for rich assholes," Slater said. "They ignore you until something goes wrong, and then you're either a hero or it's all your fault."

Rogelio looked him over. "You worked security?"

"Bodyguard jobs sometimes. I don't have a permit to carry, though. Are you armed?"

He shook his head. "Me neither. Just a baton. At that party, I stayed by the front door. The client told me not to let homeless people in. He said they'd come around because of the free alcohol."

"Which client told you that?"

"Elijah Hardin. Black guy, tall, no hair." Rogelio patted the top of his head. "I talked to a woman who works there too, Pilar."

"No one told you to watch for theft?"

"I was hired for crowd control. If you're worried about burglary, you need an armed guard. That costs a lot more than me."

"Did you see anything unusual after the lights went out?" Slater asked, watching him closely.

"People started leaving. There was more light on the street than inside. I was watching the crowd, telling people to dump their wineglasses. You can't walk around with open alcohol." Rogelio paused as a heavy truck turned into the gate of the construction site, nodding to the driver. "But I'm sure that no one came out with a package big enough to be one of those paintings."

"Did you get any weird vibes about anyone there? Did anyone stand out for any reason?"

Rogelio shrugged. "A lot of people were there for the boss. He used to be on TV."

"I see." Slater eyed him for a moment. "Don't let anyone blame you for this."

"I won't," he said, and shrugged. "I wasn't hired to protect the paintings."

Back in his car, Slater found the photo he'd taken of the police detective's card, with her name and her title in bold letters, followed by the ambiguous label ART CRIMES. Beside the text was the police department's familiar logo, rays of energy emanating from a sketch of city hall. The address for her office was at police headquarters, right across First Street from that iconic structure. He dialed her number.

"Detective Torres," she answered, and Slater explained who he was. "I need to drop by your office and ask you a couple of questions."

"I don't know," she said dubiously. "I'm pretty busy."

"I'll be brief," Slater said, raising his voice. "I'll be there in a few minutes."

He hung up before she could backtrack, then drove downtown, trolling the neighborhood around the police station in search of street parking. Eventually he found a space, fed the meter, and strode toward the building. Its security buffer meant it was deeply offset from the street. But they'd used the empty space for the best possible purpose—planting greenery.

Walking through it, he admired the brush box trees and the rush reeds. Everything they'd planted was appropriate to the climate, he saw, with no water-hungry invasive exotics. It should be that way, as the place was pretty new, and the landscaping would have been done during the drought. The *Senecio* was thriving as ground cover, but of course it would; it was essentially a weed.

At the desk inside he asked for Torres, and the uniformed cop on duty looked him over as he made the call. Torres must have decided she'd talk to him, as the guy gave Slater an office number and gestured toward the elevators.

Torres's door was open when Slater found it, and he rapped on it with a knuckle as he stepped inside. Torres looked up and rose briefly from her chair, waving for him to sit. Wearing a white blouse and gray pants, her badge attached at her hip, she looked harried, wisps of hair escaping from the tight bundle at the back of her head.

"You're the insurance guy working on the Hardin Gallery thing," she said.

"What can you tell me about it?" Slater asked, dropping into the chair in front of her desk.

"Nothing." She raised her eyebrows. "We've interviewed the principals, and the investigation is ongoing."

"What's your sense of what happened?"

"I'd have to read the file to give you an opinion, and I'm not ready to do that." She nodded to a stack of binders and manila folders at the side of her desk. "I'm working on dozens of these at once."

"So it's not a high priority," Slater said, eyeing the jumble of paper.

"Everything is top priority—but there's a lot of it."

"Do you remember if you interviewed E. L. Hardin?"

"Principal Jackson? Of course I remember him."

"Why do you call him that?" Slater said,

furrowing his brow.

"Don't you remember him from *Report to the Office*?"

"Is that a TV series?"

Torres frowned. "Where are you from, exactly?"

"I'm as much an Angeleno as you are, but I don't have a TV."

"It was a while ago, so I guess it's more of a cultural memory than part of the current zeitgeist. Hardin played Principal Jackson on the show."

"Do you have a phone number for this guy?"

"Sure," she said, and turned to her computer, tapping at the keyboard.

Slater pulled out his phone and typed the number as she recited it.

"That's his cell," Torres added.

"The staff at the gallery said they gave you the invite list for the event," Slater said, looking up again. "Can I get a copy?"

"They didn't give me anything," she said. "One of the women showed it to me on a computer screen, and I photographed it. I can't share it with you, though. It's part of the investigation."

Slater rose and pulled out his card, handing it across to her. "Can you call me if anything comes up?"

Torres eyed the card, not reaching for it, then

met Slater's eye. "It might be a while."

Slater dropped the card onto a pile of paperwork. "Just in case," he said, and walked out.

That had been an almost useless visit, he thought, walking back to his car—but at least now he had a number for Hardin.

His office was just a few minutes' drive, and he pulled into the lot, hustling across the street to his building in a break in the traffic. The day laborers were gone this late in the afternoon, and upstairs the lights were off, with no sign of Max.

On his computer Slater went to the website of the alarm company that Pilar had been using, and clicked on the button marked LOG IN. Her business card listed her email address, and he typed that in as the user name, then found the password he'd photographed on the sticky note under her desktop blotter. His assumptions were correct—when he hit Enter, he had access to the Hardin Gallery's security video archive. Just to make sure it was working, he clicked on a file from earlier today, and watched for a few seconds, realizing he was looking at himself standing there talking to Pilar. Did his voice really sound like that?

Slater sighed and clicked it off, then swung his boots up on the desk and looked at his phone, checking the tracking app for his stupid ex-boyfriend, Conrad. They hadn't been involved for all that long before Conrad summarily kicked him to the curb, but when they'd still been together, Slater had managed to install a tracking app on his phone. It was his own fault, the idiot, letting him see the code he used to unlock it. It wasn't stalking, Slater reasoned, as he needed to know where Conrad was sometimes. The guy was a shit-heel, but he was useful—as a cop he had resources that Slater needed.

Today he was out in the Valley at his house, the lazy ass. Slater dialed his number.

"I'm not at work," Conrad said when he answered.

"I can call you when it's not about work," Slater said.

"You never do that. What do you need, Slater?"

"I just met a colleague of yours, Detective Torres, downtown. Can you see if she has more info in one of her files than what she told me?"

"I can't be leaking stuff out of case files."

"She wouldn't even open it when I was there, and she couldn't remember anything about it. Just have a look."

Conrad sighed audibly. "I'll see how sensitive it is. Text me the names and dates."

Slater heard a voice in the background, the words indistinct.

"Who's that?" Slater said.

"A friend. We're gaming."

"Are you fucking him?" Slater demanded.

"You don't get to ask me that."

"I bet he's one of those Valley night crawlers. Anybody can live in the Valley, you know."

"I'm glad you understand how that works," Conrad said. "What about your nightlife? Doris said you're seeing someone."

"That's a lie," Slater snapped. "I don't do boyfriends. Not anymore. And quit talking to my mother. What would she know about it, anyway?"

"Listen, I'll be at work tomorrow," he said. "I'll see what I can find out about your case."

Slater hung up on him, huffing in frustration. Why did he have to be such a dick?

Pushing thoughts of Conrad away, he looked at his notes on his phone. The cop had given him Hardin's number, and Slater dialed it. Hardin's deep voice, familiar from watching him on the security video, answered, "Who's this?"

Slater told him his name and said, "I work for Cudahy Mutual. I'm investigating your claim for the *Hillside Roble*, and I need to sit down with you for a few minutes."

"I'm not going to be able to do that today," Hardin said. "I'm a busy man."

"You're also a man who filed a massive insurance claim. If you won't meet me, we're not even going to consider settling it. Of course, that's your choice." Slater hung up before the guy could reply. Did Hardin really think he was going to call the shots? People were so freaking stupid sometimes.

On the wall facing his desk, Slater had hung a painting he'd found in a thrift store, three faded artichokes in a bowl. They'd had a real plant in the front office for a while, a *Pothos*, but there hadn't been enough light for it. The artichokes, at least, weren't going to wither from neglect. Staring at them, Slater thought about Hardin's insurance claim. The *Hillside Roble* had cost just about a million times more than this painting.

It was odd that even though the power had failed inside the gallery, Birgit and Rogelio had both said the streetlights were still on. A while back Slater had hooked up with a line worker— but what was the guy's name, and had he kept his phone number? They'd talked about scaling utility poles, and how similar it was to the climbing skills of a pruner, both using the same kind of gear. Slater had learned how to climb trees with a harness and a belt when he'd done horticulture at college. He didn't do that kind of work anymore, except once in a while tending to the roses and bougainvillea in his mother's yard.

Gazing at his phone, he scrolled through his contacts, looking for the name. There were a lot of guys, and some had notations so that he could place them. Eventually he found a note that said "line worker." Osvaldo. That sounded right.

Thumb-typing on his phone, he sent the guy a brief text:

It's Slater. Want to hang out? My place.

Osvaldo's reply came a moment later:

I remember you. Over the cell phone store in Westlake, right?

Slater grinned and texted back:

That's me. I'll be home in an hour.

The constant sound of the sewing machines cycling on and off in the building was finished for the day as he locked up and headed down to the street, and the parking attendant was gone. Slater's place wasn't a long drive, despite the Friday traffic, just west across the chasm of the 110 freeway. The best thing about the place was the private garage, right off the alley, and after the shutter had rolled up, Slater nosed the Thunderbird inside, waiting to make sure the door rolled down completely before heading upstairs.

Two flights up was his bleak little apartment, a thrift-store sofa and a recliner in the space beyond the kitchen, with the bedroom off to one side. The paint was drab industrial beige, and the carpet bore the stains of decades of use.

On the kitchen counter stood a fifth of bourbon, suspiciously more than half empty. He couldn't remember drinking that much of it, but Slater was the only person who could have. *Not now,* he told himself, but soon enough, and stowed the bottle out of sight in a cupboard. In his bedroom he picked up the dirty clothes strewn on the floor and dumped them in the bottom of the closet, then changed into a tight T-shirt, and pulled the sheets up on his futon.

Stretching out in his recliner, he closed his eyes for a minute, thinking through the events of the day.

A sharp knock woke him soon after, and he got up, rubbed his eyes, and pulled open the door. Osvaldo had natty dark hair with a bit of gray in it, and a little mustache. He smiled as Slater pulled open the door. Such a beautiful man. Today he was wearing a heavy shirt, jeans, and boots.

"Did you come from work?" Slater asked, closing the door behind him.

"Of course I did—I punch a clock," Osvaldo said. "I don't have the luxury of setting my own hours like you do." Stepping into the main room, he said, "I forgot you lived in such a shithole."

"Welcome," Slater said, and stepped up behind him, running his hands over Osvaldo's chest and his belly. Osvaldo leaned into him, then turned around, meeting his mouth, taut and warm and intense, grasping Slater's shoulders. Slater felt his dick swelling in his jeans, and pulled him closer, hands on his waist.

Osvaldo ran a hand into Slater's hair and stepped back, chuckling.

"What?" Slater demanded.

"I forgot how sexy you were."

Slater scoffed and led him to his bed, then started unbuttoning his work shirt, running his hands over Osvaldo's warm skin, massaging his soft furry belly. Slater dropped his jeans and sank onto the futon, pulling Osvaldo on top of him. Soon they were both naked, Osvaldo's raging hard-on pressing into Slater's side.

Kissing his neck and then nibbling his ear, Osvaldo whispered, "I'm going to fuck you."

"Let's do it," Slater said, and rolled toward his bedside table, scrabbling in the drawer for a condom and lube. Slater rolled it on for him, squeezing his cock and eliciting a groan. Osvaldo grabbed Slater's knees and maneuvered himself between them, working a finger inside him, then another, holding his gaze. Eventually he penetrated Slater, then leaned in to meet his lips.

Slater gasped with the intensity as Osvaldo pounded him, exploring his firm mouth until Osvaldo came, groaning, and collapsed beside him.

"You're so beautiful," Slater said, running a hand in his hair, and then Osvaldo shifted position, taking Slater's hard cock into his mouth. Slater closed his eyes and leaned back, quickly building up tension with Osvaldo's maneuvering. Finally he came, grabbing Osvaldo's hair to stop him. Osvaldo grinned as he moved up beside him on the futon.

After he'd caught his breath, Slater slid his arm under Osvaldo's neck.

"There was a power failure at a building in the Arts District a few weeks ago. I know the DWP sent a truck. Can you find out about that?"

Osvaldo chuckled and rubbed Slater's thigh with the back of his hand. "Is that why you called me over?"

"That, plus the fact that you're smoking hot," Slater said.

"I'm working tomorrow, so I can check on the computer, if you give me the date and the service address. You could probably just phone the office and ask."

"Then I wouldn't have gotten to see you," he said.

"Things are changing there," Osvaldo said, and started talking about his job, and the work conditions, and the union, and the injustice of it all. Slater tuned him out, folding his arm over his eyes, instead enjoying the proximity and the warmth of Osvaldo's body.

Eventually Osvaldo got up, and Slater heard

water running in the bathroom. When he came back, he started pulling on his pants and said, "I have to go."

Slater was glad to hear that, and got up, following him through the kitchen and closing the front door behind him, pausing for a final lingering kiss. Before he took the fifth out of the cupboard, he sent Osvaldo a text with the date of the blackout and the address of the gallery. Setting the phone on the counter, he could now dedicate his full attention to the bourbon, hefting the bottle and admiring its hypnotic golden gleam. It was still early, but he was in for the night, so it fit with his booze rules.

As he was about to twist off the cap, his phone rang, and even though he knew he could ignore it, he saw that it was Hardin, the gallery owner. Setting the bottle down, he scooped up the phone and answered it.

"E. L. Hardin," Slater said when he picked up.

"That's me," he said, and hesitated, caught off guard. "Most people just call me Elijah, or Eli."

"What can I do for you, Elijah or Eli?"

"I realize I was hasty in not making time for you today. I apologize for that. I'm home for the evening now—if you'd like to drop by, we could have that sit-down."

Slater sighed. "It depends where you live."

"Why does that matter?"

"Because I'm not driving out to the damn beach, or to Orange freaking County."

"I live above Sunset Plaza," Eli said.

"Well, that's annoying, but I guess it's not too annoying. Text me the address—I'll be there in half an hour."

Slater had to grin. Clearly the guy had figured out that Slater had something he wanted, not the other way around. The fact that he'd called meant that Slater had the upper hand.

Back in the bedroom he pulled on his jeans and a clean shirt, eyeing the bourbon as he walked out. It would have to wait. Locking the front door, he headed down the two flights to his garage. The navigation app on his phone told him to go all the way west on Sunset, and Slater cruised the broad boulevard, through the congestion in Hollywood and on the Sunset Strip. Eventually he came to the retail stretch called Sunset Plaza. That name was typical real-estate hyperbole—there was no plaza, no open space, just sidewalks and shops and the busy road. Turning right, he drove up into the hills above.

After several more turns on the dark winding hillside streets, Slater slowed where the map told him the address was, nosing the Thunderbird into a narrow driveway. The gate had been left open, and he drove up the incline into a courtyard.

A garage stood at one side, all four doors

closed, and in front was the house, clearly intended to be grand, two stories with lots of white boards and black shingles, tacky faux columns flanking the front entrance. Slater pulled the car in a full loop in the wide courtyard, facing the driveway again, before he killed the headlights and the engine and climbed out.

The surface of the courtyard was decomposed granite that crunched under his boots, and lining the space were well-tended rosebushes and strips of bluegrass lawn. Planting that stuff was so irresponsible, even if you could afford all the water it needed. Maybe that was the point—Eli was showing his guests that cost was no object.

Before he got to the front door, Eli stepped outside, an easy smile on his face. He was taller than Slater, with hard-to-miss pecs bulging under his gray satin shirt.

"Mr. Ibáñez," Eli called in greeting.

Slater raised his eyebrows, impressed that he'd remembered his name.

"Great car," Eli continued. "What year is it?"

"It's a '78."

"I can't believe such a big old boat is only a two-door."

"It was meant to be sporty in its day," Slater said, frowning and meeting his gaze.

"Come on in," he said, and Slater followed him inside.

French doors at the other end of the foyer revealed a swimming pool, lit from below in pastel blue, the light lazily shifting with the ripples on the surface.

"I'm sure you're surprised," Eli said, closing the door behind him.

"It's a nice house," Slater said, "but I've been in nice houses before. My mother grew up in a place like this."

"I mean because it's me," Eli said, grinning and flattening a palm against his chest.

"I guess your face is kind of familiar," Slater said, cocking his head. "Someone said you were on television."

"You didn't watch *Report to the Office*?"

"I don't have a TV."

Eli eyed him closely. "I've heard rumors that people like you exist. I played Principal Jackson for nine years on a series called *Report to the Office*."

"It's a comedy?"

"Yes," he said emphatically.

"Sounds like a winner," Slater said.

Eli frowned and beckoned for Slater to follow, leading him into a living room with big windows onto the pool. Expensive-looking leather chairs faced a similarly upholstered sofa, and bookshelves lined the back wall, punctuated by a wet bar. The dark-wood floor was partly covered by an intricately patterned oriental carpet under the coffee table.

"Sit down," Eli said, and stepped over to the bar. "Do you want a drink?"

"If you're having one," Slater said, standing by the sofa and watching him.

"What's your pleasure?"

"Bourbon or scotch. Neat if it's good stuff, otherwise on ice."

Eli chuckled but didn't reply, and soon turned toward him, handing him a tumbler. Eli dropped into one of the chairs, and Slater sat opposite, on the sofa.

The glass had an inch of amber liquid in it, free of ice, and Slater took a tentative sip. It was a delicious nutty scotch.

"Damn," Slater said, "this is the good stuff."

Eli laughed, clearly flattered. "You know, it's weird to meet people who've never seen the show. It feels like being broke, or not speaking the local language, or trying to get things done in places where money doesn't mean anything."

"Where would that be?" Slater said, eyeing him and taking another satisfying sip.

"I was in Peru once, way out in the jungle, trying to get a ride down the river. Nobody would take my money, and I sat there for three days. I felt completely powerless."

"Why didn't they want your money?"

"They said the water level wasn't safe, or whatever. I got out of there eventually."

"Isn't it liberating just to be a regular person sometimes?" Slater said.

Eli shrugged, and Slater took a satisfying mouthful from his tumbler before setting it on the coffee table.

"Tell me about the night of the theft," Slater said.

Eli's face clouded, and he waved his hand as if to brush it all away. "It was a party. I introduced the painting, then mostly I just chatted with people."

"Why didn't you have a guard on it?"

"I did have security."

"On the door, not on the ten-million-dollar painting," Slater said.

"There were more people than we expected. It's a busy neighborhood."

"Where were you when the lights went out?"

"Standing in the middle of the room, talking to my guests."

That fit with the video, Slater decided, at least the part he'd seen, although the recordings ended well before the blackout.

"Was anyone acting suspiciously? Anyone who seemed out of place?"

"There were so many people." He sighed. "I didn't see anyone wearing a ski mask or brandishing a pistol. I was engrossed in enjoying myself."

"Among your guests, who do you think might have done it?"

Eli shrugged. "I don't know."

"I need to see your invite list. Your staff lied to me about it—said they didn't have it."

"I'm sure they're just being protective of the gallery," he said, his brow furrowing. "I'll have them show you." He watched Slater for a moment, then leapt up, striding over to the bookshelf. "Want to see my Emmy?" He pulled the golden statue from a shelf and held it up triumphantly, then waved languidly with his free hand, mouthing "thank you" to the empty room.

"Is that something about television?" Slater asked.

Eli scowled and carefully set the statue back in its place. "It's *the* thing about television. Christ, do you live under a rock?"

Assessing him, Slater rose, and put his hands on his hips. "I guess as far as your business goes, yeah, I do."

"This is an industry town, and entertainment is the industry. I can't believe you're that ignorant of it."

"You'd be surprised how much goes on in this town that has nothing to do with television."

Eli eyed him. "I'm not sure why, but I'm not

even that offended by your obtuseness. You're working the whole butch thing," he said, circling a palm toward Slater. "Hot but dumb—I guess that gives you a pass."

Slater's eyes narrowed. Normally he'd punch the guy in the face for making that kind of slur, but he suppressed the instinct. "Are you hitting on me?"

"I'm happy that you noticed," Eli said, and cracked a smile.

Slater stepped toward him, watching him carefully. Eli's cockiness quickly evaporated, concern clouding his expression, his muscles tensing. But he stood his ground. Stopping in front of him, his chest just inches from Eli's beautiful pecs, smelling his musky cologne, Slater reached up and put his hand on the back of Eli's neck, pulling him into a kiss. Eli went with it, and started to relax, then got into it, wrapping his arms around Slater's shoulders and pressing against him. Slater could feel his raging woody.

Eventually Eli pulled back, breathing heavily. "I really want to sleep with you."

"I picked up on that," Slater said, raising his eyebrows.

"The thing is, I need you to be discreet. I'm not public about my private life."

Slater knew he should take that as a sign— he needed to keep his dick out of his work, and sleeping with this guy was the opposite of that.

"So you're closeted," Slater said.

Eli scowled. "I'm not—I just don't want you running down the hill to talk to a gossip website first thing tomorrow, or posing for the paparazzi in my driveway."

Slater scoffed. "First I'd have to remember the name of the TV program you were in. I guess I could find it online, but it's not something I committed to long-term memory. Then I'd have to double-check for your surname in the insurance paperwork. I know it's in there somewhere."

Eli watched him for a moment, his chest heaving. "You're kind of a prick, you know that?"

Slater grabbed his waist and pulled him close. "I know that. And you know that I want you."

Eli groaned and kissed him again, then pulled away and led him back to the foyer, then up the curving staircase and into a bedroom. It had tan-colored Berber carpet and a view over the pool.

"You should see this in the daytime," Eli said, stepping over to the windows. "There's a gorgeous view of the canyon and the hills." He picked up a snow globe from the vanity by the window and gave it a shake. "Don't you love this? It's snowing in Hawaii. It's funny because it doesn't really snow there." He looked at Slater. "Where's your drink?"

"Eli," Slater snapped. "Focus."

He must have heard that before, because he said, "Right, right," and nodded, then stepped toward him.

Slater sat on the bed and pulled him down onto it, unbuttoning Eli's shirt and running a hand over his abs.

"Your body is basically perfect," Slater said quietly, and Eli preened, pushing his fingers through Slater's hair.

Slater shifted position to unbutton his shirt, glancing at the snow globe on the vanity, the last of the snowflakes still swirling over Diamond Head. Something tugged at his awareness, and he paused, looking again. Next to the snow globe was an analog clock, in a round white case with a black dial, facing the bed. Eli pulled on his shoulder, but he shook him off.

"Hold on," Slater said, and stood up, grabbing the clock. He'd seen one of these before. Examining it closely, sure enough, there it was—a little hole with the glint of a tiny lens.

"What's wrong?" Eli said.

Slater dropped the clock onto the carpet and stomped on it with the heel of his boot, shattering the plastic case with a sharp *crack*.

"Dude—what the hell?" Eli demanded, sitting up.

Stooping and pulling apart the broken bits,

Slater found the memory chip, and held it up.

"You videotape all your dates?" Slater demanded.

"Video?" Eli's eyes grew wide. "That was a camera? I thought it was a clock."

Slater stepped close to him and slapped his face, on one side and then the other, a rapid kovac.

"Ow," Eli cried, cringing, and held his cheek.

Slipping the card into his pants pocket, Slater headed for the stairs.

"I didn't know," Eli called after him, his tone plaintive.

Based on his reaction, that might be true, Slater thought, walking out the front door toward his car and buttoning his shirt. But then again, he was a professional actor. And if it wasn't his camera, who was spying on him? That wasn't really Slater's problem, but he certainly wasn't going to hang around—there might be another camera hidden in that bedroom.

Twisting the key in the ignition, Slater revved the Thunderbird's throaty engine, and popping his foot off the brake as he pulled out, spit a little decomposed granite across the bluegrass toward the house. Just a little, though, to express his displeasure; he didn't want to shatter any windows.

Cruising the streets back down to Sunset, even though Slater was lost in thought, he noticed that a pair of headlights behind him made several of the same turns. They were those stupid white-beam lamps, the outer set bright, the inner ones useless decorative illuminated rings. He didn't know what make the vehicle was, but in this neighborhood it was probably new and high-end.

It wasn't too odd that a car followed him down to the boulevard, he decided. Stopped at the red light, he got a look at the vehicle in the rearview mirror—it was a white BMW, its driver invisible in the dark interior. Just in case, Slater pulled out his phone and made a note of the Bimmer's tag number, tucking his phone away again when the light changed.

As he drove through West Hollywood, the Bimmer hung back, staying behind him no matter how leisurely Slater drove. Maybe the driver was just out cruising and happy to follow, but he changed lanes when Slater did, sometimes letting another car or two get between them, but never falling too far back. No, whoever was driving the Bimmer was definitely tailing him—he just wasn't trying to lie low, or didn't know how to.

Nearing the 101, Slater accelerated through a yellow light and took the turn onto the ramp fast. In the rearview the Bimmer blew through the red to keep up, accelerating down the ramp behind him. Interesting that he wasn't even trying to be discreet, Slater thought, and jumped into the next lane, accelerating and weaving around the traffic. It was reckless to drive like a knucklehead, he knew that, and the Highway Patrol would be happy to cite him for it if they noticed, but he wanted to see what the BMW would do.

The car kept up, not moving as adroitly as Slater, but that thing had a big engine and was crafted for maneuverability. It followed him off at Alvarado. *You're on my turf now*, Slater thought, and in his own neighborhood he knew exactly how to shake this sloppy tail.

A few blocks from his apartment, Slater pulled into a one-way alley, headed the wrong direction, ignoring the DO NOT ENTER sign. It was a reasonable gamble that he wouldn't meet an oncoming vehicle, as the alley was in use mostly during business hours for the shops on either side. At the far end of the block was a busy boulevard, and Slater stopped there, ignoring the traffic streaming by in front and watching his mirrors for the Bimmer. Sure enough, it pulled cautiously into the alley, crawling toward him.

The traffic on the boulevard had cleared, held up by a red light at the next intersection. As the Bimmer drew up behind him, Slater watched closely as the light turn green and two lanes of cars started toward him. At the last possible moment he punched the accelerator, roaring across all the lanes and into the alley on the other side. No way could the BMW get through that heavy line of traffic; he would have to wait until the light changed again.

By that time Slater was on the next street, and after making a couple of turns, keeping an eye on the rearview, he was satisfied that he'd lost the BMW. Navigating to his own alley, he waited for the garage door to roll up, scanning both directions before he pulled inside.

Climbing the stairs, he mulled the incident. Who would be following him from Eli's place? Surely the dreaded paparazzi wouldn't be staking out the home of a has-been actor; that was just Eli's wishful thinking. He could look up the plate tomorrow, he decided, eyeing the fifth of bourbon on the counter as he stepped into his apartment. For now he wanted to forget all about extroverted Eli and his short attention span.

Admiring the golden gleam of the contents, Slater uncapped the bottle and drank from it, relishing the burn in his throat, coughing at the heady fumes in his nose. Already he could feel his mind starting to slow down, the warm glow slowly suffusing his consciousness. Pouring a tumbler full, he grabbed an ice cube from the freezer and dropped it in, then stretched out on the sofa, smiling to himself. After another deep drink, he set the glass on the carpet and put on the radio. Friday-night house music fit with the mental slowdown, lulling him toward oblivion.

Eli was hot, but so damn flaky. Why were so many actors like that? Could he be that clueless as to let someone plant a camera in his bedroom? And the fact that he thought Slater was dumb actually worked to Slater's advantage—it meant Eli was underestimating him, which gave him more room to maneuver. Slater couldn't have sex with the guy, he knew that. Sleeping with Eli was just asking for trouble.

FOUR

It took a minute for Slater to wake up and realize the noise he was hearing was the ringing of his phone. Scrabbling for it on the bedside table, he saw that it was Osvaldo. Squinting at the screen, he checked the time before he picked up.

"You're up early," Slater said.

"I've been at work since sunrise. It's not early anymore," Osvaldo said. "I looked into your power failure. We did send a rig, but it wasn't a problem with the DWP lines. It was localized to equipment in that building."

"But your crew fixed it, didn't they?"

"I'd say we found it, but there was nothing to fix. Someone tripped a breaker on the switchgear."

"Tripped it? Meaning they overloaded it?"

"No, man," Osvaldo said. "Like they opened

a cabinet in the electrical room and turned off a big old breaker switch. It knocked out power for the whole building."

"So it was intentional," Slater said, half to himself. "The equipment room was open when I was there yesterday."

"The report said the switchgear was in a common access room. That means multiple customers need to be able to get in there. Sometimes the landlord just leaves it unlocked because it's easier. The cable and phone lines are probably in the same room."

"What time was the initial report?"

"Twenty-one twenty-three," Osvaldo said. "That's nine twenty-three p.m."

Slater stifled the urge to snap back at him that he knew how to parse military time, instead saying, "Excellent information. You're the man."

"Don't wait so long to call me next time, *cabrón*."

Swinging his feet onto the floor, Slater forced himself out of bed. In the kitchen he looked in the fridge, even though he knew there was nothing inside except a jar of peanut butter, some pickles and olives, and a stack of ancient take-out containers of salsa. He ate a spoonful of the peanut butter and found a ripped-open package of Oreos in the cupboard. His feelings about Oreos were ambivalent, but they were incidentally vegan, and almost nothing else on the snack shelves at the liquor store was.

After he'd put on a clean shirt, he decided his jeans were OK for another day, then pulled on his boots. Grabbing his satchel, he trotted down to his garage. The Hardin Gallery wasn't far, and the Saturday morning traffic was light. When he parked and walked up on the place, the sign hanging inside the door read CLOSED. Stepping back under one of the sidewalk carob trees, he checked the gallery's website on his phone. Opening time was ten, and it was almost ten now.

Slater walked along the facade and around the corner to the offices that shared the building. The jumbled pile of dockless rental scooters looked even bigger than it had yesterday. It was hard to see how those were a positive advancement. Piled in gutters and on street corners in trendy neighborhoods, they looked like the rusting shopping carts abandoned in the river, only these were blocking the sidewalk.

The door with the green bird logo was locked when he tried it, but the other one, Thoughtful Disruption, was open, and he stepped inside. Except for the security camera pointed at the entrance, the place looked like a kindergarten, with furniture and posters in bright saturated colors, toddlers' building blocks scattered on the front desk, and instead of chairs, big plastic balls arrayed around the conference table. Two more rental scooters lay abandoned against a wall.

A twenty-something guy stepped out of a back office and looked at Slater over his little round glasses. Clad in a tweed vest and cravat despite the heat, he wore an absurd mustache, curled up at the ends, like a nineteenth-century banker.

"You've got a delivery for me?" he asked.

"I'm not the help," Slater said, furrowing his brow, "so you can drop the condescension. I'm looking into a burglary in the gallery next door. Were you here on the evening of the seventeenth?"

"Who knows?" he said, gesturing vaguely. "We keep flexible hours."

"There was a forty-minute power outage. You would have noticed."

His eyebrows shot up. "I remember that. No one was here, but the cameras were messed up. I had to reboot all the computers that morning. It really pissed me off."

Slater put his hands on his hips. "It sounds like you're not a fan of all forms of disruption, then."

The guy frowned. "What?"

"It says 'disruption' on your front door," Slater said. "I know you're trying to reformulate the world in here, but it doesn't look like you're exactly overcapitalized yet." He nodded to the conference table. "Those ball chairs, for example.

They look a little … cheap."

"We have feelers out for venture capital," he said, his brow furrowing.

"Well, if you need some inspiration, you should try the insight technique of the ancient Greek mystics. Have you heard of them?" Slater patted his stomach. "You stare at your own belly button, and if you can focus on it for seven days straight, a brilliant beam of light will shoot out of it, providing all the answers you need."

The guy looked mystified, and Slater walked out, grinning to himself. Yanking the guy's chain was satisfying, but more significant, nobody had been here during the robbery.

Back around the corner, in front of the gallery, Birgit was wheeling her way up the ramp, wearing a sleeveless white top, her arm muscles glistening. Twisting her keys in the door as Slater approached, she pushed it open, and the alarm started beeping. Slater grabbed the door for her as she wheeled inside, stepping in after her. The gallery was too warm, the air funky, tainted by the sweet acrid scent of wood rot.

Birgit rolled over to the panel on the wall and stood up from her chair to deactivate the alarm. Stepping noiselessly to one side, Slater was able to see the four-digit number she punched in. Interesting that she can stand, Slater thought. It meant that he couldn't rule her out as the person who'd caused the power outage, even though the electrical equipment was down a set of stairs.

He pulled out his phone to make note of the alarm code. It was foolish of her to let him see it, but maybe that just meant she was guileless, or maybe that she just didn't care.

"You're certainly a persistent fellow," Birgit said, eyeing him and rolling around behind her desk.

"I am when people don't tell me the truth," Slater said.

Birgit raised her eyebrows, holding his gaze, but didn't speak.

"Show me the electrical room," Slater said.

"Show yourself," she said. "It's in the back hall. You have to use the stairs, so I can't actually take you there."

"I just saw you stand up, sister."

"That doesn't mean I can climb stairs, dumb-ass," she snapped. "Pilar will be in today. Talk to her."

Birgit rolled over to the front door and flipped the CLOSED sign to OPEN, then propped the door open with its built-in doorstop.

"You're not afraid of homeless people wandering in?" Slater said.

She sighed. "We pay extra fees to the BID to have patrols. You must have seen them in the neighborhood—they wear green shirts and ride around on bicycles. They keep the homeless west of Alameda."

"Even after dark?"

"Especially after dark. That's when the neighborhood is busiest, with all the bars and restaurants. It's also when homeless people tend to put down roots."

That was a different story than Rogelio had given him, but he didn't press it.

"Besides," Birgit continued, rolling away, toward the back door, "I need to have the doors open. It stinks like old building in here, and the HVAC has been on the fritz all summer. I'm going with natural ventilation until Pilar gets around to fixing it."

"Why hasn't she done anything about it yet?" Slater said, strolling after her. "Cash-flow problems?"

"I don't know anything about that," she said, and found the key on her ring to unlock the back door, folding down the doorstop and leaving it wide open. "If you're going to the equipment room anyway, can you prop open the door to the alley? It has a stop on it like this one."

"Sure," Slater said, and walked toward the back hallway, glancing at the oil paintings, Los Osos and the sequoias flanking the empty spot for the *Hillside Roble*. Leaving the wall empty definitely drew attention. At the end of the hall he pushed on the crash bar of the heavy outside door, glancing around at the deserted alley and kicking down the stop to prop it open.

The equipment room was still unlocked, and he flipped on the light to see there were only six steps down—it wasn't a full basement, just partly below street level, and there were no windows. Four big utility boxes with ducts running into them lined the wall. A smaller cabinet with a padlock on it was marked FIBER. The room was mostly open space, and surprisingly free of clutter. But it was a shared space, meaning no one would use it to store their own stuff.

The electrical boxes had doors on them, and he wondered if he should look inside. None of them were marked as hazardous, just as ELECTRICAL with the lightning-bolt logo. He wished Osvaldo were here to show him what was what. Tentatively pulling one open, he found a set of a dozen circuit breakers.

At the top of the steps, the door swung open, and Pilar stepped in, today wearing pants and a dark-blue blouse, her long hair bundled behind her head.

"Are you looking for the source of the power failure?" she asked, walking down the stairs.

"You neglected to tell me that someone came down here and flipped a breaker that night," Slater said.

Pilar frowned. "I didn't know that. How would I know that?"

"Didn't the DWP crew tell you what had gone wrong?"

"I never talked to them. I had bigger problems."

"OK," Slater said evenly, eyeing her.

"I know our breakers are in that one," she said, pointing to one of the cabinets, "and the one at the end has the shutoff for the whole building."

Slater stepped over to it and pulled open the door. A large switch was mounted horizontally at the top, clearly marked OFF and ON at each end. Closing it again, he turned to Pilar.

"Who could have come down here?"

"We don't lock the room, so conceivably any-one who was in the gallery, or even people in the neighboring offices."

"The opening party was at night," Slater said. "Weren't the offices closed?"

"They work at all hours. It's the tech indus-try, right, so they're more like frat boys than white-collar drones."

"So you didn't see anyone headed down here from the party?"

Pilar sighed. "If I had, I would have told the cops." She turned and walked up the stairs, call-ing back to him, "Is that all you needed?"

"For now," Slater said, following her up. "I'll show myself out the back way."

The alley was paved in ancient pot-holed asphalt, broken to rubble in places, stubby weeds poking up in the cracks. It looked disused, with only two gates onto it that he could see. Most of the properties lining it presented high blank walls, although a couple had fire doors. Most of them bore blotches of newer paint where the graffiti had been painted out. On the few lots where there was a fence, it was invariably topped by coils of razor wire.

Outside the back door, three parking spaces were vaguely outlined in faded yellow paint, one of them occupied now by a dark-green Honda. On the wall in front of it was a red-lettered sign admonishing NO PARKING: TOW AWAY, but it would be easy to stop here to make a delivery—or to load up after an art heist. Scanning up the wall, the gallery didn't have any cameras here, and none were visible on neighboring buildings either.

Walking back around to the street and his car, Slater's phone buzzed in his pants. It was a text from Conrad:

At the station until 6. Drop by.

It had better be something important, making him drive over there, Slater thought, climbing into the Thunderbird.

Despite his irritation at being summoned, Rampart wasn't really that far, on the other side of downtown, near his apartment. Slater pulled into a street space out front and texted Conrad:

I'm outside.

Climbing out of the Thunderbird, Slater stretched his back while he waited. When Conrad finally came out the front entrance, he waved Slater toward the accessibility ramp, out of earshot of anyone coming or going. As he walked over, Slater eyed him, today wearing his black uniform, barrel-chested even without a ballistic vest under it. His dark hair looked longer, like he was growing it out, with a bit of a wave in it now. It still looked sharp, and it suited him. Conrad flashed a smile as Slater approached. Such a beautiful man.

"You look rested," Conrad said, looking him over.

"Man, do not start with me," Slater said.

Conrad put his hands on his hips. "Are you off the sauce?"

"Fuck you, Conrad," he spat. "Why am I here?"

Conrad chuckled. "I had a look at that file you wanted—the digital part of it, anyway. The detective hasn't done much yet, but she made notes about her interviews. Nobody she talked to seems to know anything."

"That's what I came up with too."

"There was an invite list for the party, but she

hasn't interviewed anyone on it yet. It's mostly names with email addresses."

"Can I see it?" Slater said impatiently.

"I'll email it to you. I also ran a records check on the people she did interview, the gallery staff. Two women."

"Pilar and Birgit? Good thinking. I'm almost impressed with your initiative."

"Neither one of them has a police record."

"What about the gallery owner?" Slater said.

"Principal Jackson?" Conrad said, raising his eyebrows. "I never even checked. I figured his life is so public, if he'd been arrested or come in front of a judge, it would be all over the gossip sites."

"That's all you got?" Slater said. "You could have told me this on the phone."

"I could get in trouble for snooping around in other people's work like that," he said, frowning. "Show some gratitude. Besides, I wanted to see how you're doing."

"That's none of your damn business. Not anymore."

Conrad nodded, a thin, sad smile on his face. "I'm just glad you look OK."

"Well, you look like an idiot. You always have," Slater said, and turned to leave.

"You're welcome," Conrad called after him.

"Get a haircut, you damn hippie," Slater shouted over his shoulder. It didn't make any sense, he knew that. Slater's own hair was longer than Conrad's. But it was all he could think of to get the last word.

Climbing into his car, he saw that Conrad had disappeared, back inside. Why was he so freaking pushy? Dick-smack Conrad, telling him how he looked. Look at your own damn self, chump.

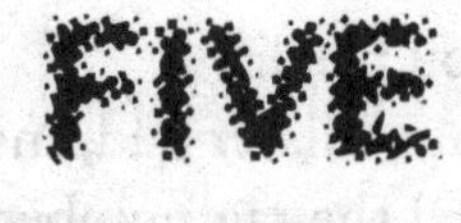 FIVE

By the time he got to the office, he'd forgotten about Conrad. Pulling on his satchel, nodding to the parking attendant, he headed across the street and into his building. It was quieter today than during the week, but even on Saturday lots of the factories were humming with activity.

The lights were on and Max was parked at his desk when he went in, wearing the seersucker suit that Slater had helped him pick out, today with a bright-yellow knit necktie. Slater had never seen that before, but it fit, a good contrast to the blue-and-white fabric. Max's girlfriend must have given him that, or taken him shopping. It was a relief, in a way, that someone else was helping him dress so that he didn't look like a low-rent bouncer, even though playing the heavy was exactly what he did on lots of his gigs.

"Nice tie," Slater said, dropping into the chair in front of his desk.

"Thanks," Max said, sitting up a little straighter.

"I'm glad you're here. Do you have a minute to do some research?"

"What do you need?"

"To run a plate," Slater said, and pulled out his phone. He recited the tag number, then watched as Max pecked at his keyboard with his stubby fingers, peering at the computer screen.

"A white BMW?" Max said finally.

"That's it. The moron tried to tail me home last night."

Max eyed him. "You managed to ditch him?"

"Easily—he didn't know what he was doing."

Max nodded, turning back to the screen. "It's registered to a car dealer. That one over by the 405."

"Does that mean it's leased?"

"Leases show up under the lease holder's name," Max said, frowning at the screen. "It's not an unsold car either, because it has a plate. Sometimes fleet vehicles are registered to a company, but most cars come back with a person's name. I can't explain it."

"The dealer is something, at least," Slater said, even though it wasn't really enlightening. Digging in his satchel, he pulled out the business

76

cards he'd taken for Pilar and Birgit. "What about these two—Conrad did a criminal check, but can you get addresses?"

"E. L. Hardin Gallery," Max read, scanning one of the cards. "This is for your insurance job?"

"That's where the heist went down."

Max looked at his computer and clacked at his keyboard. "Birgit lives in Oakland."

"That can't be current," Slater said. "She's been floating around LA for a couple of months at least."

"Pilar has an address in Whittier."

"Email me that," Slater said, and scooped up the business cards, tucking them back into his bag. "So how's it going with your cheater?"

"Uneventfully," Max said, and grinned. "I'm hoping for some action today. It's Saturday night—time for nine-to-fivers to blow off some steam."

In his own office, Slater dug in the pocket of his jeans, pulling out the memory card from the camera clock he'd found in Eli's bedroom. Nothing happened when he slid it into his computer. It wasn't that it was blank—it wasn't even connecting. Maybe he'd broken it when he stomped on the clock.

Checking his email, he found the party invite list that Conrad had copied from Detective Torres's file. It was several grainy and distorted photographs of the information on a computer screen, but the names and contact details were legible. Slater read through them, not recognizing any names, then spent a few minutes searching for several of the people online. One was an actor that he'd never heard of who had been in a couple of vapid-sounding superhero movies; another was an art collector who had endowed a local college; then a music-industry finance person.

The list was essentially useless, Slater decided, staring at it on his screen. These people were just wealthy Angelenos, potential clients of the gallery rather than potential thieves.

Shifting focus, he went to the alarm company website and logged in with Pilar's credentials to look at the security videos. Osvaldo had given him the time that the DWP had been called for the power outage, but how long before that had the video coverage ended? The time stamp at the end of the last video, just before the lengthy gap, was eighteen minutes before the DWP call—that was so long that it was pointless even to study the footage to see who might have been absent from the party.

Slater sighed. From these recordings, it was impossible to tell who had turned off the breaker. The camera covering the hallway would have taped anyone walking into the electrical room, but that clip was lost. Maybe whoever had done it knew that the last few minutes wouldn't make it into the cloud.

Closing the alarm company page, he opened another to do a search. The web had an excessive amount of information about Eli Hardin, Slater found, and he spent a minute reading several breathy biographies.

Eli had worked on that TV series for nine years. It looked teen-oriented—the marketing photos depicted smiling youths in front of brightly colored school lockers. Eli had grown up in Beverly Hills, which was surprising—Los Angeles was heavily segregated along racial and class lines, and Beverly Hills had very few black residents. Eli's father had been in the film industry, one website said, and like his son, he'd been an actor, appearing frequently in small roles in serious films rather than on television. That explained why his parents had the resources to live in a wealthy white enclave, but not why they had chosen to do that.

Slater looked up at a sharp knock on the front door.

"You expecting anyone?" Max said, stepping out of his office and adjusting his jacket to cover his holster.

"No," Slater said, locking his computer with a keystroke and rising from his desk.

Max pulled open the door. "Can I help you?"

Not waiting for an answer, his tone softened. "Hey—aren't you Principal Jackson?"

"I'm not," Eli said, a big grin on his face, "but I played him on television." Today he was wearing a purple polo shirt and snug dress pants that showed off his pleasing curves.

"That was such a great character," Max said. "He brought a lot of joy to the world. I'm Max, by the way."

"Thank you so much for saying that, Max," Eli said, shaking his hand.

Watching them from the doorway of his office, Slater frowned. He'd never seen the sycophant or the fan boy come out in Max before.

"The role gave me great pleasure too," Eli said, and glancing at Slater, added, "There's the man I came to see."

"Am I the only person on the planet who didn't watch *Report to the Principal?*" Slater said.

"It's *Report to the Office,*" Max said.

"Of course," Slater said. "That's completely different."

Max had pulled out his phone. "Can I take a selfie with you?" he asked. "I want to show my girlfriend."

"I'd be delighted," Eli said, and leaned in as Max held up his phone, wrapping an arm around his shoulder and smiling beatifically at the camera.

After it flashed, Max pulled his phone down and studied the screen. "We both look amazing," he said, and then to Slater, "I have to head out. I got a surveillance video hit."

"It was nice to meet you, Max," Eli said, as Max stepped past him.

After the door closed, Slater said, "You certainly know how to work your fans."

"It's almost a full-time job."

"How did you find me?"

Eli shrugged. "Online. Your name is associated with this address."

Slater folded his arms. "OK," he said neutrally.

"I wanted to apologize for last night," Eli said, his tone earnest, holding Slater's gaze. "I didn't know about that camera, I swear. I'm just as freaked out about it as you are. I spent an hour going through the house in case there were others. Someone must have planted it there."

"Who?" Slater demanded.

"I have some ideas, but I'm not sure yet. I'm looking into it."

"You think your house cleaner is working for a gossip website?" Slater said. "Or maybe someone in your entourage wants to out you?"

Eli scowled. "I'm not closeted," he said, raising his voice. "I'm just private about my private life."

Slater put his hands on his hips. "It's interesting, though, that straight people in the public eye never say that. They're always tits-out about who they're fucking."

"That's not true."

"Anyway, if it wasn't your camera, someone is spying on you—I'd be worried."

"I just said it wasn't me," Eli insisted. "Why don't you believe that?"

"Why would I believe you? The whole thing is hinky."

"So distrustful," Eli said, and sighed, closing his eyes and rubbing the top of his head. When he looked at Slater again, he spoke more calmly. "You took the memory card with you last night."

"It's not working. I must have busted it when I disabled the camera."

Eli nodded. "The other reason I dropped by was to invite you to a small gathering I'm having tomorrow afternoon at my house. It's Sunday, so Bellinis and mimosas. It'll be fun."

"Seriously?" Slater said, frowning. "Why do you want me there?"

"I think you know I'm interested in you."

Slater watched him for a moment. "How many people will be there?"

"It's hard to predict. Friends of friends usually come, so maybe thirty to a hundred?"

"That's not exactly small," Slater said. "But sure, I'll swing by."

"Great," Eli said, grinning. "There'll be valet

parking." He dropped his chin and fixed Slater with an intense gaze. "I'm glad you're coming," he said quietly. "I very much enjoyed what we started."

With that, he turned and left, closing the door behind him. Slater stared at it for a moment, still smelling his musky cologne. Eli could be dazzling when he wanted to be. Maybe he really was a talented actor.

Ducking back into his office, he pulled on his satchel, waiting inside the front door until he heard the elevator rumble open. Quickly locking up the office, he headed to the stairwell. The elevator was old and languid, and he knew he could catch up to Eli if he hustled down the stairs.

Sure enough, when he got out to the sidewalk, Eli was just crossing the street toward the parking lot. As Slater watched, Eli strode toward a dark-blue sedan. A Bentley. Of course he was driving a freaking Bentley.

Slater waited until he had climbed in and pulled onto the street, then sprinted across and got into his own car. It wasn't hard to tail the Bentley, as Eli drove leisurely and kept to main streets. Slater hung back a block or so, letting vehicles get between them and changing lanes, staying out of sight. Eli didn't have far to go, navigating to the Arts District and soon pulling into the alley behind his gallery. It was completely uninformative for him to come here, Slater thought. Following him had been a waste of time.

Parking the Thunderbird a block away, Slater walked into the alley. The Bentley was in one of the marked spaces behind the gallery, beside the green Honda. The crash door from the hallway was still propped open, the way he'd left it for Birgit this morning. Moving as quietly as he could, Slater stepped inside. The doors to the neighboring offices were closed, but at the end of the hall, the door to the gallery was open. Such lax security—that camera up above wasn't much of a deterrent.

Voices drifted into the hallway, and Slater stopped, standing flat against the wall, out of sight of the front desk. Pilar and Eli were talking, maybe upstairs in one of the little offices. They both sounded angry, their voices growing louder.

"You need to nut up and take care of this," Pilar said.

"I've got bigger problems," Eli shouted.

"Ten million dollars' worth?"

"I trust you with this stuff," he snapped. "Do your damn job."

"You're never around," she said. "That means I'm doing your damn job too."

Eli didn't reply, but Slater heard footfalls on the metal stairs. He turned and headed out to the alley, glancing back as he ducked out to make sure he hadn't been observed.

Walking toward the side street, he was almost at the sidewalk when a dark-red SUV roared by, moving fast. At the wheel was Pilar, sunglasses on, hunched intently over the wheel. She didn't notice him, it seemed, and he watched as she turned at the next corner. He didn't need to follow her, he decided, or even write down the plate number—he knew where she lived.

Sitting in his car, he glanced in the mirrors to make sure he was alone, then checked his email for Max's message, the one with Pilar's home address in Whittier. His navigation app told him to take the 60, and he started the engine, pulling out and heading that way.

The late-afternoon traffic wasn't bad on Saturday, and soon he was off the freeway and cruising the boulevard, then turning into a low-slung leafy neighborhood. Pilar's place was a mid-century bungalow with a short iron fence fronting the quiet street. English ivy covered the fence's brick pillars. Why did people plant that stuff? Turn your back for a hot minute and it was out of control, up the wall, eating the shingles. It was already starting to swallow a citrus tree inside the fence. It looked like an orange, or maybe a grapefruit, and it had been there for a while, maybe as long as the house had. The neglect was infuriating.

The red SUV wasn't in sight, but a ratty green

Camry, missing a front wheel cover, was parked in the driveway. Slater slowly cruised past, then did a U-turn at the next corner and parked across the street, a few doors down, facing the house. Reaching into the backseat, he found his binoculars, lifting them to his eyes and surveying the place.

There were no cameras that he could see, and no alarm-company signs. One of the neighboring houses, with newer paint and sleek drought-tolerant landscaping, had a camera aimed at the front walk, but Pilar's driveway wasn't in its line of sight. As he panned the house, an Anglo-looking woman with streaky blond hair stepped out the side door, opened the driver's side of the Camry, and threw in her backpack. She looked to be in her thirties, and wore jeans and a long-sleeved white shirt.

At that moment the red SUV pulled in beside it, and Pilar climbed out, a grocery bag in one hand and her keys in the other. Pausing briefly to kiss the blond and exchange a few words that Slater couldn't hear, she went into the house. The blond climbed into the Camry and backed out, driving toward Slater, who dropped the binoculars and shrank back in his seat.

She didn't even glance at him or the Thunderbird, and Slater fleetingly considered tailing her. No, he decided, Pilar was the target. It felt like the blond lived there, which meant she had to be Pilar's wife, or girlfriend. You'd think lesbians would be smarter about taking charge of the landscaping.

Daylight was fading as he scanned the house again, wondering whether it was worth waiting here—Pilar could be in for the night. It would be easier just to put a tracker on her car, but doing that in her driveway was risky, as he could easily be observed. Maybe he'd swing by the gallery tomorrow and find her car there.

But then the side door swung open, and Pilar stepped out, now wearing a colorful dress, her hair loose and free-flowing. She'd redone her makeup too, with heavier eyes and dark-red lipstick. Climbing into her SUV, she backed out, driving past Slater and heading toward the boulevard.

Once she was out of sight, Slater cranked the engine and turned around, heading after her. Not sure which direction she'd gone on the main street, he gambled and went toward the freeway, and soon enough saw that he'd come the right way—she was getting on the 605. The SUV was easy to follow, as it had a weird aftermarket taillight bar along the top that glowed in a distinctive bright cherry red, unlike the standard warm red of the sea of other taillights.

Pilar drove fast, transitioning onto the 60 at breakneck speed, but the Thunderbird easily kept up. As they approached the snarled interchange with the 5 in Boyle Heights, Slater had to veer across a couple of lanes to follow her off at a short exit. For a second he thought he might have lost her again, but then he caught sight of the cherry taillights up ahead, cruising past Hollenbeck Park.

The SUV turned onto a residential street, and as Slater followed a minute later, he saw it was already parked, in a driveway behind two other vehicles, its rear end blocking the sidewalk. A cluster of balloons was tied to the front gate of the house. This was an old part of town, with small lots and narrow streets, and as he crawled closer, a car pulled away from the curb just across from Pilar's vehicle. It was much closer to his target than he wanted to be, but finding anywhere to park in this dense cramped neighborhood was practically a miracle. Besides, Pilar had never seen his wheels.

Pulling into the street space, he killed the engine and shifted downward in his seat, hoping the deepening twilight would make him invisible.

The balloons implied there was a party going on, but no one was in the front yard, and the driveway was deserted. The house was tiny and had bars on the windows. Out front grew a spindly avocado tree with fruit on it, and closer to the house were low oleanders. Not bad choices if you didn't have time to worry about your yard.

But there were signs of life, he saw, watching

two young women and a man walk up to the gate. They closed it behind them and went to the side of the house rather than to the door, disappearing in the gloom of the narrow space along the fence. The action must be in the backyard.

In the driveway Pilar appeared again, accompanied by a woman, older than her and dressed for a party, in a bright patterned skirt and heavy makeup. Slater cracked his window to overhear them. They were speaking Spanish, peppered occasionally with English phrases. Finally Pilar said, "It won't take long," and climbed into her car.

The red SUV backed out, and Slater rolled up his window, slouching lower as she passed. Hand poised on the ignition, he watched the cherry-red taillights recede in the rearview for a moment, but then jumped when someone rapped on his passenger window. A twenty-something woman stood there, bent over to look inside. In the darkness he hadn't seen her approach.

Slater frowned and reached over to crank down the glass a few inches. "What's the problem?"

"It looks like you're scoping out my house," she said, pushing her hair back and peering in at him. "Are you looking for someone?"

It would be easy to blow her off, but it would be less suspicious to talk to her—especially since she could identify his car.

"I was going to meet Pilar here," Slater said,

"but I think I missed her—she just left."

"She'll be back," the woman said, and smiled. "Don't be shy. You should come in."

"Why not?" he said, and rolled up the window, then pulled his keys out of the ignition and climbed out.

SIX

"I'm Norma," she said, glancing up the street before stepping across. "I'm sure Pilar has told you all about her family."

"I haven't met anyone," Slater said, following her through the gate, "so I'm not clear on all the names."

"I'm her little sister. It's my birthday—didn't she tell you that's what the party was for?"

"Happy birthday, Norma," Slater said, and grinned to himself as she led him along the side of the house.

In the backyard, tables were set up, and a dozen people were scattered around, some seated, some standing, talking over the pop music playing on a pair of little speakers set up on the food table next to the back door. Several big foil trays were arrayed next to plates and forks, and two drink dispensers sat beside a stack of plastic glasses. Both dispensers were clear and looked like they contained lemonade, but one had a plastic mustache taped on the front—that had to be cowboy margaritas.

"We haven't really heard about you," Norma said, stopping in front of the drinks. "What's your name?"

"I'm Slater."

"You should meet our parents," she said, and beckoned for him to follow.

Slater already knew who they were, based on where they were sitting, in the lawn chairs at the back of the yard, right in the center, positioned like the honored elders. Norma spoke to them in Spanish, and he knew he was being introduced. The only words he caught were his own name and *novio*. He knew what that word meant: *boyfriend*. Norma grinned at him and stepped away. Her mother's eyes lit up at *novio*, and she gave him a thoughtful once-over. Clearly Pilar's family didn't know about the blond with the Camry.

"*Buenas tardes*," Slater said, and then greeted the father, briefly gripping his hand and mumbling "Nice to meet you" before he retreated.

Walking over to the food table, he ignored the skanky *carnitas* and loaded a paper plate with a still-warm tortilla and rice and beans. After he grabbed a fork, he stood at the side of the yard to eat and survey the crowd. A couple of people greeted him as they came in along the side of the house. Slater waved his fork or nodded in acknowledgment. Norma was nowhere to be seen, but soon a woman in a print dress approached him. She looked more like Pilar than Norma did.

"I'm Lupe," she said, and extended a hand.

Slater palmed his fork and delicately shook her hand, then introduced himself.

"Norma said you're Pilar's boyfriend," she said. "I wonder why I've never heard of you?"

"I was wondering that myself," Slater said. "So how do you fit in?"

"I'm Pilar's older sister," she said, eyeing him critically. "I work for a bank. Fraud detection."

"I bet you'll be keeping an eye on me, then," he said, and winked at her, then took another mouthful of rice.

Lupe looked puzzled, but said, "Have a margarita. I made lots. Later, Slater."

He rolled up his tortilla as he watched her walk away, toward her parents at the back of the yard.

The place was filling up and getting louder, the conversations almost drowning out the music. Everyone looked like family, with similar Latin features, and most of the discussions were in English. Slater didn't really stand out like an interloper, although he got a few curious glances.

Stepping over to the food table, he dropped his empty plate into the trash, then pulled a plastic cup from the stack and filled it from the mustachioed dispenser. It was sweet, and tart, and strong with tequila—clearly Lupe knew what she was doing.

The blond woman he'd seen at Pilar's place appeared at the side of the house, walking into the backyard and stopping to talk to Norma. Slater couldn't hear what they were saying, but the blond's expression shifted, glaring at Slater as Norma pointed him out. He slammed the margarita and dropped the cup into the trash, glancing around to assess where the yard's points of egress were. Just in case.

Her expression guileless, Norma walked over with the blond, who now had murder in her eyes.

"Jill wanted to meet you," Norma said. "Slater, this is Pilar's roommate. I'm surprised you two haven't met before."

"I've heard so much about you," Slater said, eyeing Jill.

A lanky teenage boy walked up to them and looped his arm through Norma's, pulling her away, leaving Slater alone with Jill.

"And I've heard nothing about you," Jill said, and lowering her voice, "Who the fuck are you?"

Slater sighed, and shook his head. "Lesbians. Always so angry."

"Why are you posing as Pilar's boyfriend?" Jill demanded.

"I never said that to anyone. Norma made that assumption. It's your own damn fault if you're closeted—you can't blame me."

"I can call the cops, though," Jill said.

"Go for it," Slater said. "Mom and Dad over there will find out the truth. In the long run that might be a good thing for everybody. I'd be happy to cop to milking the misunderstanding to score a plate of food and a cowboy margarita, but nobody's going to pop me for that."

Jill huffed in frustration. "Tell me who you are."

"I work in insurance," Slater said casually, glancing around at the party.

"What are you doing here?"

"Looking into Pilar. I'm trying to figure out if she's a crook." He met her gaze. "I know you won't tell me the truth about that, but I thought I might get a sense of it from her family."

Her eyes widened. "The gallery robbery? That had nothing to do with Pilar."

"Were you there?"

"For the party, sure. But I didn't steal anything."

"So who did?" Slater said, watching her closely.

"How should I know?"

"Were there any shady-looking people at the event?"

Jill gazed absently at the crowd, considering that. "You should look into Elijah's nephew," she said finally. "He works there sometimes."

"What's his name?"

"Tyrell," she said. "He's kind of a lost kid—out of high school but no career, no goals."

"Was he there that night?"

"Of course he was," she said emphatically. "That's why I thought of him."

"Why hasn't anyone else mentioned him?" Slater demanded.

"He's not around much. He's kind of a twinkie, so he blends into the background."

"What does he do when he works at the gallery?"

"Odd jobs, I think, and deliveries, that kind of thing. In the back room, though, not out front with the customers."

"Where can I find this kid?"

Jill shrugged. "Ask Elijah."

Over her shoulder, Slater saw Pilar walk into the yard, her face clouding with concern when she caught sight of him.

Striding over to them, she asked, "What are you doing here?"

"He's posing as your boyfriend," Jill said, frowning at him again.

"I'm not," Slater said firmly. "Norma made that up. I just didn't bother to correct her. Why are you closeted with your family?"

"You've crossed a line here," Pilar said. "You need to leave."

"I'm done eating anyway," Slater said, shrugging. "First, though, tell me where I can find Tyrell."

Pilar looked confused. "Eli's nephew? I don't have his number—not on me, anyway. He's supposed to come in tomorrow to do some work."

"I'll see you then," Slater said, and flashed a smile. "I enjoyed meeting your parents. Say goodbye to Norma for me, and tell Lupe her margaritas are the bomb."

Pilar scowled as he walked away, but no one accosted him on his way out to the street. A couple of people greeted him on their way into the backyard, and when he glanced over his shoulder as he went out the front gate, no one was tailing him.

Across the street, he opened the trunk of the Thunderbird and grabbed a vehicle tracker. It was an exquisitely effective but extremely illegal surveillance tool he bought from the Russians in Glendale. Hiding it in his palm, he slammed the trunk and surveyed the street, looking for the red SUV. Not finding it, he walked to the end of the block and onto the cross street, then went into the alley. All the gates and garages were closed, several with security lights that winked on as he passed, but his instinct had been right—Pilar's car was pulled up tight in front of a white garage door. This had to be right behind the family house.

Walking up on it, he could hear the party on the other side, loud voices and tinny music. Scanning the dark alley for obvious security cameras and observers, and finding none, he found the recessed power switch on the tracker and slid it on with his fingernail, then crouched beside the SUV, reaching up into the rear wheel well. It took a little maneuvering, but eventually he found a steel surface, and the tracker's magnets adhered to it with a satisfying *click*. Standing up again, he scanned the alley and made his way back around to the Thunderbird.

As he climbed into his car, a vehicle cruising the street stopped behind him, turn signal on, eager to obtain such a vanishingly rare parking space. Slater started the engine and turned on his lights, relinquishing the spot and driving a few blocks to the boulevard, where he pulled over again at a red curb, leaving the engine running and killing the headlights, but leaving the parking lights on. Digging out his phone, he sent Andy a brief text:

Sex?

Part of the deal with the Russians was that their gear was linked to a tracking app they'd also sold him. Despite the fact that the menus were in a clunky mishmash of English and inscrutable Cyrillic, it all worked really well, to the point that he was happy to pay the hefty subscription fee they wanted. Pulling up the app now, he found that the tracker was already on the map, in Boyle Heights, the location estimated to be within a green circle that covered the alley and three houses, including the one he'd just been at.

Rather than using GPS, the device sniffed out stronger Wi-Fi signals to determine its location, updating the app via the cell network. That made it useless in the mountains or the desert, where nobody had Wi-Fi, but it also didn't need an antenna or a view of the sky. It used far less battery power, and as long as Pilar's SUV was in the city, it would keep reporting its location for four or five days.

Svetlana, his principal contact at the clandestine Russian workshop, had explained that Wi-Fi was an ingenious way to assess someone's location, as there were two different public databases that were easily queried. Both were updated continually by taking the GPS location from people's phones and geographically pinning the Wi-Fi points that were in range. However it functioned, it usually worked pretty well, and saved Slater the trouble of stakeouts and tailing people.

On the web, he searched for "Jill" with Pilar's

address. The name came up on a real estate site—Jill and Pilar jointly were the most recent buyers of the house. As he made note of Jill's last name, his phone buzzed with Andy's terse reply:

I'm here.

Turning his lights on again, Slater pulled into the traffic and headed for the First Street bridge, paralleling a brightly lit metro train on the long expanse as he cruised over the river into downtown. Enough work for one day—he wanted to spend some time with the beguiling Andy. Unlike so many people, the guy took Slater at face value, didn't tell him what to do, didn't want to fix him.

Pulling into the surface lot beside Andy's building, he paid the attendant the flat evening rate and headed for the front door. It had once been a warehouse, recently converted to lofts, but it retained the airiness of its industrial past, with concrete floors and high ceilings.

As he stepped off the elevator into the hallway, he passed a guy walking away from Andy's door—twenty-something, dark-haired, with a scruffy beard and jacked arm muscles. He nodded to Slater as he passed, swinging the long flat case he held in one hand. Andy's was the only door this far down the hall—the guy had to be coming from there. Slater turned to watch him walk onto the elevator, studying his athletic butt and the black case. It was too big to be a briefcase. Maybe it was for artwork. Whatever was inside, it looked heavy.

Slater banged on Andy's door, and it took him a minute to come and open it. Dressed in boxer shorts and a T-shirt, his brown hair a perfect tousled mess, Andy smiled as he stepped in.

"Who the hell was that just leaving here?" Slater demanded, following him into the loft. The glittering towers of the Financial District were visible in the darkness beyond the multipaned windows.

"That's Ted," Andy said, turning back to face him, his random twitching not betraying anything more than serenity.

"Who the fuck is Ted?"

"Why are you angry? You have no … claim on me. I'm not your boyfriend—I can hang out with whoever I want. I know you're sleeping with … other people."

Slater could feel his chest heaving. "Tell me who he is."

Andy glanced down at Slater's hands, which he'd unconsciously curled into fists. "Are you going to punch me if I don't?"

"I'm going to go punch him." He paused, glaring, and then slammed the wall with the heel of his fist. "I mean it," he snapped.

"Such a hothead," Andy said, scowling. "He's

a massage therapist. My muscles are a mess, and he helps me a lot."

Watching him, Slater took a deep breath, and decided he believed him. The black case could have been for a massage table. "Why do you have to have a masseur who's good-looking and buff?"

Andy laughed. "I asked, but they were all out of unattractive people. Besides, a masseur has to have the strength to get through my muscles. Do you know how thick the gluteus is?" He stepped toward Slater, his gait uneven but his intention clear, and wrapped his arms around his waist. "Relax," he said, and kissed him.

Slater leaned into it, relishing his firm inviting mouth. Just a moment of this and he could forget all about the masseur, and cowboy margaritas, and nineteenth-century art. It had taken a while to get used to it, Andy's random movements and twitching, but they'd worked it out, and Slater knew how to touch him now, and how to respond.

The loft was essentially a studio, the only internal walls near the front door, for the bathroom and a closet, and they were standing near Andy's bed. Andy pulled Slater down onto it, fumbling with Slater's belt. Eventually he managed to get it unbuckled, and Slater slid his jeans down, sitting up to pull off his boots. Turning back to Andy, he climbed on top of him and let his weight settle on Andy's torso, his woody pressing into him, the way he knew turned him on.

After a minute Slater rolled off, and pulled Andy's shirt over his head, then unbuttoned his own. When they were both naked, Slater moved down and took Andy's rock-hard cock in his mouth, working it gently. Andy drummed his fists on Slater's head, not hard but ramping up in intensity as he got closer. When Andy exploded, he grabbed a fistful of Slater's hair to make him stop. Once he'd caught his breath, Andy climbed up on him and grabbed his cock, stroking him until Slater came too.

Slater shifted alongside him, rolling one arm under Andy's neck and folding the other over his eyes. The warmth of Andy's body, his random motion slowly cycling down, just being next to him—it felt so comfortable, so right. This was almost as good as bourbon.

"I'm a little nervous about ... meeting your mother on Monday," Andy said, pulling Slater out of his reverie.

"You don't have to be. Doris is pretty laid-back."

"What should I wear?"

"It doesn't matter," Slater said. "It's just a courtesy intro. You don't need to invest too much in it."

"Still, I want to look decent."

"So wear a shirt with a collar. She was a teacher. Educators are always pro-people, right, so she'll like you no matter what you wear." Slater lifted his arm and met his eye. "Listen, I need info on a couple of people for a case I'm working. Maybe you could hack them for me."

"I don't hack," Andy said flatly.

"Well, whatever you call it—just get whatever you can."

"What case is this for?"

"Cudahy Mutual is on the hook for a painting that got jacked from a gallery. I feel like I'm stumbling around in the dark because there's absolutely no evidence, just a roomful of people who didn't see anything."

"You have all their names?"

"I just need you to look at the gallery staff. One of them was on a TV program, a guy named E. L. Hardin."

"Elijah Hardin?" Andy said, eyeing him. "Principal Jackson? No way am I going to try to get into his stuff. Hacking celebrities is a whole other … ball game. People do hard time for that."

"I'll pay you more."

"No way," Andy said. "Nonfamous people only."

Slater scoffed and sat up, reaching for the floor and finding his phone in the pocket of his jeans. Snuggling up to Andy again, he emailed him the names and contact info he had for Birgit, and Pilar, and Jill.

Sometime later he woke. His nose was in Andy's hair, and he had one arm around his belly, his thighs nested into the curve of Andy's. Gently extricating himself, he sat up and started to get dressed, pulling on his shirt.

"Stay," Andy said softly, shifting onto his back.

"I slept over on Thursday."

"You're going home to get drunk."

"That's not your business," Slater said.

"You can drink here."

"I wouldn't do that to you," he said, and rose, stepping into his jeans.

"You're afraid I'll try to make you go sober."

"I'm not afraid of you," Slater said gently, sitting beside him again and caressing his bare chest. "Fuck, you're beautiful."

Andy held his gaze, and said intently, "I know who you are."

Slater didn't reply, pulling on his boots and heading for the door. He wasn't so sure that was true.

⁕

A surprising number of people were walking the streets, considering how late it was, and Slater navigated out of the parking lot toward his apartment. He knew what was waiting for him—that bottle of liquid gold. Part of what made Andy tolerable was that he never pressed Slater to quit drinking, which Conrad and Doris did regularly. Andy was in recovery himself, going to meetings, working the steps, sponsoring other junkies, the whole enchilada, so he probably knew that pushing Slater to do anything like that would backfire.

Climbing up the stairs to his apartment, the only thing in his mind was the fifth in the kitchen cupboard, and he grinned to himself when he found it, waiting for him, constant and immutable and perfect. He cracked the seal and guzzled from the bottle, relishing the burn in his throat, then poured himself a tumbler, dropping an ice cube into it, and stretched out on the sofa.

It was late, but there was no urgency to get to bed; everyone slept in on Sunday. Taking a slurp from the tumbler, he set it on the mottled carpet and put on a podcast that he listened to sometimes, *Sasquatch Search*. Slater's feelings about the hairy cryptid were ambivalent, but following the team on their quest into the boreal woods took him out of the everyday. Even now he could feel his mind unwinding, along with the narrator trudging deeper into the forest, sinking toward unconsciousness.

His head throbbed when he woke up, and he smelled bad, that sickly sweet tang of the by-products of digested booze. He was naked and in his own bed, but he had no memory of how he got here. Where was his phone? Not on the bedside table, or in the drawer when he pulled it open and scrabbled around inside, or on the floor when he felt for it there.

Sitting up, Slater had to pause, rubbing his temples and waiting for the nausea to subside. Eventually he could stand, and went into the bathroom, shaking some ibuprofen into his mouth from the little bottle, then washing it down with a tumbler full of tap water from the kitchen sink.

Deep breath. His laptop, at least, he could

find, in his satchel, tucked behind the sofa. Usually he only hid it there when he had a hookup coming over, but he hadn't done that last night. Had he? He tried to remember. No, he'd been with Andy, and got home late.

Sinking onto the sofa, he pulled open the laptop and squinted at the screen. Using a tracking app, he told it to ring his phone, and sure enough he could hear it, faint and muffled but somewhere in the bedroom. When he went to find it, the sound was coming from his closet, and he shifted a pile of dirty clothes, finding the device right at the bottom, face down on the floor. He must have hidden it from himself, not wanting to drunk-dial people.

It was still morning, he saw, and there were a couple of alerts from the Russian tracking app, telling him that Pilar's car was moving around. He'd deal with that later. Tossing his phone on the bed, he went to the kitchen and ate a spoonful of peanut butter and a couple of Oreos, which tasted way too sweet for some reason, and a vegan Pop-Tart.

The ersatz food made him feel better, and he had a shower, then got dressed, in a decent black shirt with a collar. Rosa had even ironed it. She came in every couple of weeks to clean up as best she could, even though the grime in the carpet and around the tub was undeniably permanent.

Eventually she'd taken pity on him, or maybe got sick of picking up dirty clothes to vacuum under, and started doing his laundry. He had to pay her more for that, but it was worth every dime.

Stuffing his phone into his jeans, he grabbed his faux-leather jacket—he was going to a party today, after all. It was too hot to wear it now, so he folded it over his arm as he left, trotting down the stairs to his garage.

There was no traffic on the way downtown, and the parking lot was empty, without even an attendant on duty yet. His building was deserted and quiet, the factories closed on Sunday. Unlocking the office, he flicked on the fluorescent lights and scanned the place, ducking his head into Max's office to make sure it was empty before setting his satchel on his own desk.

Once he was sitting, he opened the Russian tracking software and checked on Pilar. The history of her location had some gaps in it, as the technology wasn't perfect, but it was clear that she had driven from her parents' place to Whittier late last night, presumably to her own house. The car hadn't moved for nine hours, but now it was farther east, near Riverside. As he watched, the circle on the map jumped and resized itself as software somewhere calculated the device's location. It went gray for a few seconds now and then, indicating uncertainty. Each time it moved, though, the circle still intersected the 60 freeway. Pilar was on the road, but where was she going?

His phone buzzed, and he picked up when he saw it was Andy.

"What have you got for me?" Slater said.

"You treat me like a tool."

"You're getting paid."

Andy chuckled. "I managed to access the texts and … voice mail for Jill. I couldn't get into any of the others."

"Right on," Slater said. "How did you manage that?"

"Don't ask. Jill's voice mailbox was empty, except for a robo message from her dentist, but I got about six weeks' worth of texts. It's all pretty boring. She doesn't say anything about stealing your painting."

"Leave the analysis to me," Slater said. "You're not a detective."

"Neither are you, hot stuff. I'll email it to you now."

After he hung up, Slater found the message from Andy. He'd put the texts into a spreadsheet, hundreds of rows of short messages, each one with a date and time, but he soon realized it wasn't Jill's full conversations, just one side of them—her outgoing messages only, responses unknown. He sighed, scrolling through the sheet. This wasn't optimal.

Looking at the texts she'd sent this morning, one stood out as informative:

On our way to the desert. Be back tomorrow.

That explained why Pilar's car was out near Riverside—there was plenty of desert in that direction.

Slater checked the spreadsheet for the rows time-stamped the evening of the heist, and the day after, scanning the messages. Jill had sent a lot of ambiguous replies, "OK" and "Not yet" and "Will do," the requests unknown. But then one jumped out at him:

Got it. 20 g's richer, baby.

It had been sent three days after the painting went missing, in the evening. Slater could feel his heart pounding, staring at her words. Had Jill sold the *Hillside Roble*?

Pulling up the alarm company's website, Slater logged into Pilar's account and found the video files from the evening of the opening party. Jill was there, he saw, her botched peroxide job glaringly evident even at this grainy low resolution. She stood close to Pilar, briefly caressing her back at one point and leaning in for a kiss. Unlike at the family party, at work the pair of them obviously weren't afraid to show people they were together.

Twenty minutes before the end of the video

coverage, long before the lights went out, Jill left, walking out the front door past Rogelio, and didn't appear on either camera again. Still, that didn't mean that she wasn't involved in the heist.

Looking through more recent video, from yesterday and this morning, the gallery was mostly quiet. Birgit sat at her desk, sometimes showing clients the paintings, but there wasn't a lot of foot traffic. Not long after she'd opened the place this morning, a skinny dark kid walked in the front door and spent a minute talking to Birgit. His hair was in a stylish knobby do, and his tight pants accentuated his slight frame. Birgit went back to her computer, ignoring him as he strolled across the gallery space and went into the back room. This had to be Tyrell.

Looking back through the surveillance videos from the opening party again, Slater found that Tyrell had been there too, as Jill had said. Briefly interacting with Eli early on, he floated around the periphery, chatting with other people.

At one point he went to the bar and spoke to the bartender. The words they exchanged were drowned out by all the other conversations, but Tyrell pulled a card out of his pocket and handed it to the bartender, who studied it for a second before handing it back. As Tyrell tucked it into his pants, the guy poured a glass of wine and handed it to him. It must have been his ID—Tyrell was old enough to drink, but didn't look like he was.

Pausing the video when Tyrell was facing the camera, Slater studied his features, trying to parse his expression. He needed to talk to this guy.

Flicking off the lights and locking up his office, he went down to the street and across to his car. The attendant was here now, along with a few more vehicles, and he waved to Slater as he climbed into the Thunderbird.

A few minutes later he was trolling the streets of the Arts District for a parking place. It was much busier than during the week, with pedestrians crowding the sidewalks and waiting in clusters outside restaurants. It made sense, he had to admit, that people who could afford to eat in these tony places would have to be somewhere working during the rest of the week.

Finally he found a meter and pulled in, locking his car and walking the couple of blocks to the gallery. Birgit was on her own at her desk, and frowned at the sight of him as he stepped inside.

"You must love coming in here," she said.

"Good morning to you too," Slater said. "Where's Pilar?"

"I think she went to Palm Springs for a couple of days."

"That sounds dumb. It's not going to be nice out there for another month or two. Right now it's hot as hell."

"I wouldn't know," Birgit said. "I suggest you take it up with her."

Slater folded his arms. "So her and Eli—do they see eye to eye? About business, I mean."

Her eyes narrowed. "Not always."

"I know they argue."

"Eli's never here, but he expects things to be done in a certain way." She gestured dismissively. "Anyone who has a boss will tell you the same story. You can either be quiet and resentful, or work it out verbally."

"What specifically do they disagree on?"

"I don't know," she said irritably. "Listen, Eli told me to show you the invite list from the party."

"I thought you'd given the only copy to the police detective," Slater said.

Ignoring that, Birgit worked her computer mouse, staring at the screen. Eventually she twisted it around, revealing a list of names and contact details.

"Can you email it to me?"

"I can't, but you can photograph it—like that police woman did. There's about three screens' worth."

Slater pulled out his phone and took photos of the list, gesturing for her to pull up the next part.

Once he was finished, he slid his phone into his jeans and asked, "Who prepared this list?"

"Pilar did, with Eli's input. They're all his people."

"Is Tyrell here today?"

"Who told you about him?"

"Are you going to tell me, or do I have to go look for him myself?"

She frowned. "He's in the back room."

Slater threw up his hands. "How difficult was that?"

Strolling back into the gallery, he eyed the oil paintings as he passed, towering sequoias and rocky Los Osos flanking the glaring blank spot. Under the catwalk, he pushed open the door marked PRIVATE. Tyrell was standing at the table with a metal bar in his hand, a piece of blank white canvas and more hardware arrayed in front of him. He was wearing the same kind of skinny pants Slater had seen in the security video, and short-sleeved blue plaid, unbuttoned to the middle of his bare chest. Definitely fuckable, Slater decided, assessing him.

"Who are you?" he asked, looking up.

"I'm an insurance investigator," Slater said. "I'm looking into the *Hillside Roble*. You're Tyrell, correct?"

"Most people call me Ty. What do you need from me?"

Slater put his hands on his hips. "Did you steal it?" he demanded.

Ty smirked, unperturbed. "No, unfortunately. I wish I had—it would be fun to cause that much chaos."

"People were upset?"

"Everyone was freaking out. It's what I'd call high drama." Ty looked pointedly at Slater's chest, and dropped his eyes to his crotch. "You look like you might know a thing or two about that."

Slater chuckled. This kid was cocky, and he was definitely flirting.

"Do you have time for lunch?" Slater asked. "I'm buying, but you have to pick the place."

"I just got here. I've got work to do." He paused, dropping his chin and raising an eyebrow. "But I'll be done in a couple of hours."

"What are you doing here, anyway?" Slater said, waving at the table.

Ty frowned, as if it should be self-evident. "Framing art, man."

"Did you frame the *Hillside Roble*?"

"Are you kidding me? That was Eli's baby. I never got near it."

"How does framing work?"

His eyes narrowed. "I thought you knew about this stuff."

"I'm in insurance, not art."

"Well, you measure the canvas, then cut these rods to the right size." Ty waggled the metal bar. "Usually there's already some that will fit." Reaching with the bar, he tapped a flat box at the end of the table. It contained a jumble of similar pieces. "The canvas gets stretched—carefully, as Eli always says—and then attached with these clips. Traditional frames were made of wood, and they were decorative. This is a modern technique that shifts the emphasis to the artwork rather than the frame."

"Can I watch you do one?" Slater asked.

Ty nodded and picked up a screwdriver, setting to work, grabbing the components from the box on the table. The metal clips were ingeniously designed, he saw, to bind the canvas to the metal framework without piercing it. Ty deftly positioned them and pulled the canvas tighter. The end result was a simple metal border around the painting, like the ones hanging in the gallery. It was true that the minimalist frames put the emphasis on the painting—he'd barely noticed how the ones hanging on the walls were framed, focusing instead on the art.

Eventually Slater had seen enough, digging in his pocket and dropping his business card on the table. "Text me when you're ready for lunch," he said, and went to the door.

In the gallery, Birgit was talking to a man and a woman, her wheels parked in front of one of the paintings, depicting Half Dome in Yosemite, mounted on the wall opposite the sequoias and the blank space for the missing *Hillside Roble*. They looked moneyed, the woman with well-coiffed hair, the man in shiny loafers and a tweed jacket, despite the heat.

"How invested are we, as viewers, in the landscape?" Birgit was saying. "The transformation of our understanding requires a dialectical relationship with the work—a willingness to embrace the constellation of archetypal structures the artist has allowed us to share. What do we, as viewers, feel when these concepts are stripped raw, exposed to the core?" She glanced at Slater as he walked past, her delivery unwavering. He had to grin. Whether anyone was buying this stuff or not, Birgit was a slick huckster.

The day was warming up when he got outside, and his black shirt felt warm in the bright sun. Once he was in the Thunderbird, he blasted the air-conditioning for the trip back to the office.

Max was at his desk when he got in, his holster strapped on over a white shirt, his suit jacket folded over the back of the other chair.

"How's your cheater?" Slater said, standing in his doorway.

"You know what they say about Saturday night," Max said.

"Everybody cuts loose on Saturday night?"

Max grinned. "I got most of what I needed.

Next I have to talk to the client and break the bad news."

"Wear your red suit," Slater said. Max cut an intimidating figure in red, which meant his client would be more likely to pay up. "So how would you feel about helping me check out a residence tonight? One of my targets is away for the evening. The only problem is, I don't know if there's an alarm. There aren't any cameras or security signs outside."

"As long as it's later on—I'm having dinner with the girlfriend."

"That's still Vanessa? You've been with her for a long time."

"Of course it's still Vanessa," Max said flatly. "It's only been a couple of months."

"That sounds like an eternity. You're not bored?"

Max scoffed. "Not everyone needs as much variety as you do. So where is this place we're visiting?"

"East—Whittier. Can I meet you here after dinner?"

"Deal," Max said.

Slater loved that about him, that he was always up for the work, always eager for an adventure, however illicit it might be.

Dropping into his chair in his own office, Slater opened the photos he'd taken of the party guest list on Birgit's screen, and then pulled up the images Conrad had found in the police file. Looking at them side by side, they seemed to be identical—except for one entry. Angela Hayes. The name was on the list that Detective Torres had, but it was missing from the list Birgit had shown him. Slater double-checked, making sure that was accurate, that the name hadn't just been shuffled to another position on the list. But he was right: Birgit's version was one entry shorter.

A web search came up with a raft of people who had that name, but the most likely candidate was a film producer. She lived in LA, worked in Eli's industry, and that job title meant she had access to money—exactly who Eli targeted for the gallery.

Reading a bio for her provided an unexpected detail: Angela had actually been married to Eli. Slater pulled up other sources to check, but it seemed to be true. They had divorced three years ago. There were no children, and the terms of the split were confidential, the gossip journalist in a trade paper explained, but the estranged couple planned to maintain a healthy working relation-ship. It was a puff piece, so who knew what their relationship was really like. Regardless, Angela Hayes definitely merited a closer look, especially if she'd been at that reception. Most interesting was that Eli had been married to a woman, but he was trying to get into Slater's pants.

Farther down the page, the photo of Angela showed her smiling, the wrinkles around her eyes putting her at least in her forties. She looked thin, and had short African hair. Using Pilar's log-in on the alarm company's website, Slater checked the videos again. Angela had been at the party that night, he saw, looking leggy in heels and a white pant suit. She talked to Eli for a few minutes, amicably enough, it seemed, considering he was her ex, although in the noise of the crowd Slater couldn't hear what they were saying.

Next she wandered around languorously, studying the art, chatting with a couple of people, getting a drink at the bar, and then talking to Pilar. She was still in the gallery when the videos ended, but that didn't mean much. Far more compelling was that she had been deleted from the invite list between the time they'd shown it to the police and when they'd shown it Slater. If they were trying to hide Angela from him, he needed to dig into her.

In his pants his phone buzzed, and he pulled it out. The sender showed as just a phone number, with no associated name, but Slater knew who it was:

Pick me up in 15 minutes. I'll be out front.

"Later," he called to Max as he walked out, then headed down to his car. When he drove up in front of the gallery, Ty was there on the street, wearing big dark sunglasses, standing in the shade of one of the carob trees and gazing intently at his phone.

Rolling to a stop, Slater tapped the horn, and Ty sauntered over, stooping to look in the passenger window. He pulled down his sunglasses, probably just for dramatic effect, to meet Slater's eye.

"Sweet ride," he said, and pulled open the door to climb in.

"I know," Slater said. "Where are we going?"

"There's a breakfast place near here. Two blocks up and then left. It might be busy, though—it's tweaker time."

"Not yet," Slater said, pulling away from the curb. "That starts at two. Is it even a thing around here? I thought it was more about WeHo."

"You really are gay," Ty said, looking at him. "I wasn't sure at first."

Slater scoffed. "I'm glad we cleared that up."

Pulling into a parking stall in the narrow lot beside the restaurant, they climbed out and walked toward the entrance, where half a dozen people were waiting for tables.

"You like the food at this place?" Slater said, eyeing the crowd as they approached.

"I've never eaten here," Ty said cheerfully. "I've only seen it."

Stepping inside, Slater asked the host to put them on the list. When she asked for his name, he said, "John Slade."

Back out on the sidewalk, waiting with the others, Ty pulled down his sunglasses and shot Slater a look. "That's not what you told me your name was."

"Why would anyone use their real name in public?" Slater said. "Any lowlife within earshot could identify you."

"That's exactly the opposite of what Eli says."

"What does Eli say?" Slater said, folding his arms.

"You should always speak your name, and say it loud and proud. That way everyone will know who you are."

"In his industry, that makes sense," Slater said. "But not in mine."

The place was bustling, but there were lots of tables turning over, and before long they got seated near a window. Slater ordered the lone vegan option, avocado on sourdough toast, and Ty asked for two full entrées from the brunch menu, along with two sides. After the waiter was gone, Ty swiveled in his seat, his eyes bright, checking out the other clientele. Watching him, Slater suppressed a grin. He might be of drinking age, but he was still such a kid.

"Tell me about the opening," Slater said. "What

happened when the painting went missing?"

Ty's expression turned serious. "I had a couple of glasses of cabernet, so I was a little tipsy. I was crushing on this industry guy, a real looker, in a suit and tie, but he disappeared. Suddenly the lights went out. At first no one freaked out, because there were emergency lights. People were laughing, and moving out onto the street. Then everyone is screaming about the *Hillside Roble*."

"Was anyone hanging around it before that, or doing anything unusual?"

"I wasn't really interested in the painting. I know it's valuable, but come on—it's a picture of a tree. No one was looking at it."

When their food came, Ty's plates crowded most of the table. He dumped his fries on top of his biscuits and eggs, then dug into it with gusto.

"My mother would call you a *fresser*," Slater said, munching on his toast.

"What's that?"

"Someone who eats a lot."

Ty chuckled and focused on his food.

Once he'd finished, Slater said, "It must be nice to have a prominent relative who's out."

Ty shrugged. "He's not that out. But I guess it's not a secret either. I wish he had more free time."

"You don't get to hang out?"

"He always has his boy toys around. One at a

time, though, not all at once. I guess I cramp his style."

"But you work for him in the gallery."

"Part-time," Ty said, eyeing him. "It's not enough to get by. I have a couple of other jobs too."

Slater nodded, watching him start on his pancakes. Eli had resources—why wasn't he taking care of this kid?

"What are your other jobs?" Slater said.

"I do massage in the evenings. That pays really well." Ty flagged down the waiter and asked for a take-out box. The guy came back with one, plus a plastic bag to carry it in. Slater took the check, and Ty loaded the remaining half of his meal into the plastic container.

Digging in his pocket, Slater slipped some cash into the folder with the check. When he looked up, Ty was gazing at him, his eyes soft. Slater knew that look, knew what it meant.

"Maybe you could use a massage," Ty said. "I could show you a thing or two."

"You think?" Slater grinned at him, and set the folder at the edge of the table.

"I mean, have sex with me."

"I understood what you meant," Slater said. "I can't do that."

Ty frowned. "I thought this was a date. That's why I ordered lunch and dinner both—I figured

I'd pay you back when we got naked."

"You're too young for me. Plus it would be sleazy to sleep with someone I'm investigating."

Ty sat up, his eyes wide. "You're investigating me? Seriously? I thought you were looking for that stupid painting."

"You were there when it went missing. You already admitted it."

"So were fifty other people," he said, and bit his lip thoughtfully. "I guess I should be flattered that you think I could pull off something like that. I could certainly use the money." Scooting his chair out and rising, he said, "So if you're not going to fuck me, at least give me a ride."

Slater stood up, waiting for him to gather up his leftovers. "Where to?"

"Tweaker town," Ty said flatly, and headed out to the street.

Slater followed him to the car, and once Ty had climbed in and slammed his door, he started the throaty engine.

"It's right on Santa Monica Boulevard, by La Cienega," Ty said.

Slater pulled onto the street and headed toward WeHo, accelerating onto the 101. They rode in silence, Ty behind his big sunglasses, gazing out the window. Maybe Slater had misled him, inviting him out to eat when his real purpose was to interrogate the kid. Maybe Ty was hurt at being rejected. But Slater couldn't do anything about that.

Exiting the freeway, he drove up the ramp and turned onto the boulevard. In the distance a huge plume of smoke, gray and white, billowed up over the hills.

"That's a brush fire," Ty said.

"It is fire season."

"I heard about it on the radio. It broke out overnight in one of the canyons." Ty turned to him. "You know, I kind of love the idea that I'm being investigated. It makes me feel like a badass."

"Are you worried about what I'm going to dig up?" Slater said.

Ty laughed. "I'm not actually a badass, Slater. Looking into my life is a waste of your time. You should take a closer look at the gallery."

"For what?" he asked, glancing over at him.

"Those women who work there—Birgit and Pilar. They're both weirdos. Kind of aloof, you know?"

"I can see that."

"Pilar got all caught up in the freak-out that night, screaming and trying to block the doors, but Birgit just sat there, like she didn't care."

"Interesting," Slater said.

"It's just up here," Ty said as they drove into Boystown, gesturing in the windshield to a storefront ahead on the left.

Slater pulled over to the curb and watched as Ty opened the door, gathering up his take-out bag.

"Thanks for lunch," he said, climbing out.

Slater watched as he trotted across the street, his legs gazelle-thin in those tight pants, hustling to avoid the traffic. The sign on the place he went into read SPICY ASIAN MASSAGE. It could be a legit health business, but it sounded more like a sex thing. In this neighborhood it could be either.

Clearly Ty hadn't been invited to Eli's party, as it was time for that now. Slater pulled into the traffic and drove up to Sunset, heading west, into the hills.

EIGHT

A valet stand was set up at the bottom of Eli's driveway, and cars lined the street on either side. It was easier just to park his own wheels, and Slater drove farther up the road, to the end of the line of vehicles, and found a space, pulling in and cranking his front tires against the curb. Pulling his faux-leather jacket from the backseat, he climbed out of the car and shrugged it on. He hated how much he loved this jacket. It was such a contradiction, because he'd never buy real leather, but he loved the way the fake version looked on him.

Walking back down the street, Slater found the valet stand abandoned, and headed up the driveway. Halfway up, a guy with expensively coiffed salt-and-pepper hair and a pastel polo shirt greeted him.

"I wondered where you were," he said, and waved a little yellow card at Slater. "Come on—I have to go. It's a black Mercedes."

Slater scowled at him. "I'm not working," he said, and kept walking.

"Yo, *cholo*," the guy called after him.

Turning back, Slater was able to step right up to him—this guy was so entitled that he wasn't even expecting pushback. Slater slapped him in the face, hard left and then right, a rapid kovac. The guy stumbled backward, his expression shocked, with Slater following him.

"I am not a *cholo*," he said intently, then slapped him once again, his palm connecting with the guy's forearm as he yelped in fear and moved to shield his face.

Walking up the driveway again, Slater listened for footfalls on the decomposed granite behind him, but if Mr. Mercedes had grown angry, it hadn't spurred him to retaliate.

In the courtyard in front of the grandiose colonnaded house, the granite crunching under his boots, Slater scoffed at the stupid landscaping. Even fifty years ago, or whenever this place had been built, bluegrass had been a stupid thing to plant.

The front door was wide open, and no one was staffing it, but Slater could see through to the pool deck, where there were signs of life. He walked through the foyer and out the French doors. A dozen or so people were sitting on the patio furniture and standing around, talking loudly. A bar was set up near the French doors. Booze—that would explain the intensity of the discussions. No one was using the pool, its blue depths placid and unperturbed.

In daylight the view really was dramatic, as Eli had promised. Intermittent rooftops dotted the vegetation in the canyon below, and in the hazy distance he could make out the towers of Century City. Looking the other way, a scrubby undeveloped hillside stretched up to the ridge-line, the dramatic smoke of the brush fire rising behind it, much closer here than when he'd seen it earlier. Surely it wasn't a threat here, or the street would have been blocked.

A couple of people checked him out from a distance, curiosity in their eyes, but the bartender was the one who spoke to him.

"Would you like a mimosa?" she asked.

"How about a beer," Slater said, and she pulled out a Corona, popping off the cap and placing a little lime wedge in the top. Taking the bottle, he pushed the lime into it and took a drink.

Eli's guests didn't seem too tight, now that he'd had a minute to observe them, which made sense, as it was still broad daylight. Their vivid conversations might be less about the booze and more about the business they were in—actors always seemed to be animated. They were mostly white and Anglo, typical of the industry, and there were a couple of interesting guys, although they both looked like scenesters, with chic outfits, gym bodies, and trendy hair.

Slater stepped toward the edge of the pool. A few feet away, a man and woman were talking.

"All that smoke can't be good for your health," the woman said, gesturing at the angry gray plume with her cocktail.

"I'm just glad I don't live in that canyon," the man said. "The roads are all closed. I'd have to evacuate. How boring is that?"

Slater was watching the smoke lazily drifting east when a guy appeared at his elbow.

"Are you a friend of Elijah's?" he asked.

Slater looked him over. He had knobby black hair like Ty's, but he was older, maybe in his thirties, and wore a yellow cotton sweater draped casually around his neck.

"Might be," Slater said. "Who are you?"

"My name's Merlo."

Slater gave his own name and asked, "Where's our host?"

Merlo glanced around the pool. "He's here somewhere. It's a nice day for it, at least."

"It's always a nice day in this zip code," Slater said, nodding to the view. "Even with the fire."

"So how do you know Elijah?" Merlo said casually.

Slater met his gaze. "That's the second time you've asked me that."

Merlo looked toward the house as Eli stepped out, wearing a tight black athletic top. It was for jogging, maybe, or cycling, but it showed off how buff he was. Eli had his phone to his ear, and when he caught sight of Slater, his eyes narrowed.

Merlo stepped over to him, and soon Eli put his phone away. They might be sleeping together, Slater thought, watching them talk. At a minimum they were very well acquainted.

A lithe woman in a billowy blue sarong stepped up to them, wrapping an arm around Eli's waist, and the three of them talked for a while. Slater drank from his bottle and turned away, wondering whether it was worth hitting on either of the gay guys he'd scoped out.

Soon Eli stepped up to him and put his hand on Slater's arm, squeezing his bicep through his jacket, grinning broadly. "You made it."

"Nice shirt," Slater said, pointedly eyeing his pecs. Off to the side somewhere he could feel Merlo's eyes on them.

"So did you just slap one of my guests?" Eli said, stepping back a little, his brow furrowing.

"Why would I do that?"

"He just phoned me to complain that some guy who was working here had smacked him. He was trying to get his car. There was mention of a leather jacket."

"You think I look like an employee?" Slater demanded.

"He said it, not me."

"What did he say, exactly?"

Eli looked embarrassed, shifting his weight from one foot to the other. "He said, 'Who the hell do you have working for you? Some Mexican in a leather jacket slapped me, twice.'"

"I'm not Mexican," Slater said simply. "My father was from El Salvador."

"So it was you?"

"Your friend is probably talking about what the Russians call a kovac. Technically it's not two slaps, but one fluid movement. It's not meant to disable, just to get your attention, so it doesn't leave a mark. Some people call it the paintbrush, and in Japan it's *oufuku binta*, a round-trip slap. In your industry it's called the Joan Crawford because she used to do that to people in her movies."

Eli stared at him. "Who are you?"

"A guy who knows how to defend himself. Your guest shouldn't have shoved me. I wouldn't have had to slap back."

"He shoved you?" Eli said, his eyes narrowing.

"That's what I'll tell the cops if he files a report."

"I don't think he will," Eli said. His expression softened, and he looked around. "So do you want to meet some of my people?"

"No rush. Why aren't Pilar and Jill here?"

"Pilar is staff. These people are friends and colleagues."

"What about Ty?"

Eli scowled. "That wouldn't be appropriate either. How do you know about Ty?"

"I met him at the gallery. What's inappropriate about him? I know he wants to be closer to you."

"Ty needs to take care of himself," he said irritably. "He knows what he's doing is shady. I can't very well introduce him to people in the business when he's doing stuff like that."

Before Slater could ask what, exactly, made Ty shady, a guy walked up to Eli, touching his arm and pulling his attention away.

Slater strolled around the pool, nodding to people when they caught his eye. A blond woman in jeans and a sheer white top shot him a smile and then spoke to him.

"Did you work on *Report to the Office*?" she said.

"I'm connected to the art gallery," Slater said.

"I've never been down there," she said, raising

her eyebrows. "It's such a seedy neighborhood."

"Not anymore," he said flatly. "Where do you live?"

"Near here."

"You have to get down out of the hills sometimes, and see what the real world is like."

She looked mystified, and Slater stepped away, heading back to the bar to exchange his empty bottle. Before he could get there, he saw Eli through the window into the foyer. Catching Slater's eye and stepping back, he grinned and beckoned for him to come in.

When Slater went in the French doors, Eli was walking into the doorway opposite the living room. It was the kitchen, he saw, long and roomy, with shiny stainless appliances and an island down the middle. Eli closed the door when they were both inside, then shoved Slater back against the counter, wrapping his arms around him, gripping his shoulders through his jacket, and kissing him hard.

Slater tensed up at first, caught off-guard, but then leaned into it, running his hands over Eli's snug shirt, feeling his dick tightening in his jeans. After a minute, Eli pulled back.

"It's too bad you can't be open about this," Slater said.

"You think I'm closeted," Eli said, frowning. "I'm not. Stop saying that."

"Then why the subterfuge? Why not kiss me in front of your guests?"

"It's called discretion, Slater." He huffed impatiently. "I really want to sleep with you."

"That's not going to happen—not here."

"There are no other cameras," Eli said. "I checked."

"I can't be sure of that."

"Maybe I can come to your place, then."

"You can," Slater said, "but you're not going to like it."

The kitchen door swung open, and Eli quickly pulled back, standing with his hands on his hips.

"There you are," Merlo said, eyeing them in turn. "The bartender needs more vodka."

"Right," Eli said, nodding vigorously and avoiding his gaze. He crossed the room, pulling a bottle out of a box on the counter and then walking out.

Merlo studied Slater for a moment, and then followed Eli.

Wandering out to the bar, Slater asked for another Corona, then stepped over to the pool. The air was already getting cooler as the shadows grew longer, even though sunset was a ways off. Sunlight glinted off the distant office towers, and in the other direction the unchecked plume of smoke roiled overhead.

A woman with henna-red hair and a tight top

with a plunging neckline stepped up to him.

"I was wondering who you were," she said, cocking her head, unambiguously flirty.

"The name is Slater. I'm connected to Eli's art gallery."

"That must be an interesting business," she said, swirling the ice in her cocktail.

"What about you?" Slater asked. "Were you in *Report to the Office*?"

In an instant her demeanor shifted—her eyes flashed, and her mouth became a tight line. She threw her drink in Slater's face, the cold liquid a shock, making him inhale sharply. The ice cubes bounced onto the concrete, shattering and skittering away. His shirt was drenched. Someone gasped audibly, and conversation stopped.

Slater didn't budge, and licked his lips. "Vodka cranberry, am I right?"

"I can't believe you're still standing there," she snapped.

"I'm curious as to why that question was offensive," Slater said.

"I'm far too young for that series," she said, jutting her chin out. "I'm on the *Real Meteorologists of SoCal*."

"See, I knew you were an actor, manufacturing all this drama. Mission accomplished, toots, if you were angling to get everyone to look at you."

"I'm not an actor," she said, frowning. "I'm a

scientist. It's reality TV."

"I wish there hadn't been fruit juice in your drink. I'm going to have to get this jacket cleaned."

"Or just throw it in the trash," she said, raising an eyebrow. "It makes you look like a thug."

Slater reached up, and before she could react, planted his palm on her face, shoving her backward. With a cry of surprise, she twisted away and lost her balance, stumbling backward and falling into the pool, water splashing up onto the concrete deck. By the time she managed to stand up, she was screaming unintelligibly.

Slater stepped away, glancing around at the other party guests. Most of them were focused on the woman in the pool, but one of the gay guys, in a tattersall shirt and a natty purple tie, was staring at him.

Stopping beside the guy and looking at the pool, then leaning in conspiratorially, Slater said, "I'm no meteorologist, but I know that level of humidity can really mess up your hair."

Wide-eyed, the guy didn't reply, his eyes darting to the pool and back to Slater.

"Nothing?" Slater demanded. "Fine. Maybe I'll just go." He guzzled the rest of his Corona and set the bottle on a patio table, then headed toward the foyer.

A big guy that he hadn't really noticed before moved in front of him, blocking the French doors.

"Who do you think you are?" he demanded, scowling at Slater. "She's a national treasure. You need to apologize."

Slater looked back to the pool, where the woman was making a loud production of climbing out, aided by several people on the deck.

"I don't think so," Slater said, balling his fists. "She generated the drama, not me."

His eyes flicking down to Slater's hands, the guy stepped aside, still scowling, and Slater went into the foyer. It was probably a good thing that Eli hadn't seen all that, although he'd definitely hear about it soon enough.

At the foot of the driveway the valet stand was deserted. Lucky he hadn't bothered with them—it always happened that they got busy and made you wait.

Out on the street, when he was a few paces up the road from the driveway, he heard rapid footfalls behind him, and spun around in time to see a looming fist. Dodging sideways, the blow caught him on the shoulder, spinning his torso left. It was the big moron who had tried to make him apologize. No way was this guy going to land another punch.

Slater easily ducked his mooky attempt at a left hook and caught him on the chin with a full-force solid right, spinning his head, and then followed with a quick dick-punch. The guy crumpled to his knees, grabbing his crotch, gasping for breath.

"Why do you make me do this to you?" Slater shouted, and kicked him in the ribs, pausing, and then kicking again. The guy collapsed, face contorted, folding into the fetal position. Watching him for a moment, Slater saw he wasn't going to make any more trouble. "Idiot," he muttered, and turned away, massaging his shoulder.

Why were big guys so damn slow? Punching a bag in a gym twice a week doesn't mean you can win a fistfight. It was like their judgment faculties were as musclebound as their stupid arms.

His shirt was still damp and smelling boozy citrusy sweet by the time he got to the car, but the jacket was already dry, and he pulled it off, throwing it in the backseat. He started the engine and made a U-turn, heading down the hill to the boulevard.

———◆———

Waiting for the light so he could turn left onto Sunset, he thought about what Eli had said about Ty. Boystown was almost on his way back, and he drove that way, cruising past the shop where he'd dropped the kid. The sign for Spicy Asian Massage was lit up now, with twilight falling, the lettering glowing red and purple. Almost directly across the street was a coffee place—a good vantage point to surveille the massage joint, and it was still open. Slater pulled into a street space and jogged over in a break in the traffic.

Even though it was evening, lots of people were sitting out on the patio. Slater went in and bought a decaf soy latte, then positioned himself at a table outside with a view across the street. The neighborhood had lots of foot traffic, and as he sat there nursing his paper cup, several people went into Spicy Asian Massage. They were all guys, he realized, after the sixth one had entered, and none of them were dressed for sports—it was definitely a sex place.

Pulling out his phone while he waited, keeping an eye on the massage place, he checked his tracking app for Conrad. The dumb-ass was at that country-western dance bar in the Valley. Why was he hanging out there on a Sunday? Hitting on sweaty mindless guys, no doubt, everybody bare-chested, in tight jeans, high on cheap beer and pheromones. Fucking moron. Huffing in frustration, he pulled up the tracker for Pilar's car. It was stationary, and as expected, the map it showed was of Palm Springs, the green location marker encircling a hotel complex.

Slater looked up as another guy went into the massage joint, and then, in the dimness at the side of the building, he noticed a fire door swing open. A buxom woman in a short skirt, sleek long hair spilling around her head, stepped out and sat in one of the plastic chairs, elegantly crossing her skinny legs. The small outdoor space wasn't in view of the street, but from Slater's vantage point, he could see into it. It must be where the employees went to smoke.

Setting a plastic bag in her lap, the woman took out a food container and a plastic fork. Lifting the lid, she started to eat, pushing her hair back and biting carefully so as not to mess up her lipstick.

It struck Slater then that he'd seen that takeout box before—he'd paid for it. He was looking at Ty, dressed as a woman. Watching her eat, he thought about it. The skinny legs, the shape of the jaw—it was Ty, no doubt about it. The kid didn't seem like he was trans; he was just in drag. Dressed like that, no way was he doing therapeutic massage in there—it was definitely sex work.

In his pocket his phone buzzed, and he pulled it out to check. It was a text from Max:

Headed to the office.

Slater sighed. He'd seen enough here. He thumb-typed a reply:

Be there in 30.

Once he'd climbed into his car and pulled into the evening traffic, he thought things through.

When Eli had called the kid shady, he didn't mean he was doing drugs or robbing houses—it was about the spicy massage. Why was he judging him for that, rather than helping him find a different job?

Ty had told Slater that he worked as a masseur, just not what kind of masseur, or that he did it in drag. Even so, the kid was pretty straightforward. Slater knew all about liars and grifters and lowlifes. Nothing about him was like that. He probably wasn't capable of pulling off the art heist, he decided.

Heading downtown, he wondered if Andy's buff masseur provided similar happy-ending services. That easy dumb smile, perfect scruffy beard, jacked arms. *Do you know how thick the gluteus is?* Andy had said. Slater could feel his heart pounding at the thought of that punk touching Andy's glutes or anything else. But feeling that way about Andy made no sense, and he pushed it away.

NINE

The parking lot across from his building was deserted, and when he got upstairs, Max was in Slater's office with the safe open. It was fixed to the floor using the bolts that had been set in the concrete for that purpose a hundred years ago, although unlike their white-collar predecessors, he and Max kept mostly illicit electronic surveillance gear locked inside.

"I'm just stowing my weapon," Max said, rising and pulling his jacket back on.

Slater nodded. That was smart—there was a big difference between breaking into a house and breaking into a house with a gun. Max was also wearing his ugly brown suit, the one that Slater hated, but that was calculated too, as he never wore it, and it was generic, making him less recognizable.

"I assume we need the key kit?" Max said, and crouched in front of the safe again, pulling out the heavy binder full of master keys.

"The jammer too," Slater said. "I don't know if there are cameras inside, so we'll wear caps."

Max set the jammer, a heavy square metal box, on Slater's desk. "Do you want to wear coveralls? If we get challenged, we could say we're plumbers."

"That might be hard to believe at this hour. Let's just be careful."

After he loaded the key kit and the jammer into his satchel, Slater went into the front office and took two blue ball caps off the coat rack, stuffing them in as well.

"So what are we looking for, exactly?" Max said.

"It's a painting—not very big." Slater pulled out his phone and found an image of the *Hillside Roble*, passing it to him.

Max studied it for a moment. "Why is this worth ten million bucks?"

"Something about the tech-industry gold rush. The world is a strange place sometimes."

"You're telling me," Max said, frowning at the screen. "It's a picture of a goddamn tree. Didn't you say the cop you talked to was in art crimes? The real crime is that this piece of crap is worth more money than I'll see in my lifetime."

Chuckling, Slater took his phone back.

Max locked the door as they left, and in the elevator, asked, "Do you want me to drive?"

"That would be great," Slater said, and they walked across to the parking lot and climbed into Max's matte-gray Challenger.

"Where are we headed?" Max asked, shifting into Drive and aiming for the street.

"Whittier. Get on the 60," Slater said. "So how was your dinner date?"

"Great. I knew it would be an early night—Vanessa has a presentation in the morning."

"I wondered about that. You're getting some action once in a while, I hope."

"I've got no complaints," Max said.

Slater eyed him, saw the trace of a grin on his face. "Damn—it must be hot."

Max laughed. "I'm a lucky man."

"I have so many questions."

"Do you really want the details?"

"Good point," Slater said.

Sunday evening traffic was light, and soon they were climbing the hills in Montebello. Even though they were surrounded by the metropolis, the curve of the freeway up the undeveloped ridge was out of view of the city lights, and for a few minutes it felt like the true darkness of the countryside.

"Who knew Whittier was so far away?" Max said.

"It's not that far. Get on the 605 south."

With Slater's directions, Max soon pulled onto Pilar's street, and parked near the end of the block.

"That's the house," Slater said, pointing it out. The green Camry with the missing wheel cover was in the driveway, illuminated by the light over the side door. He knew where the red SUV was—safely out in the desert.

"No alarm?"

"I'm not sure about that," Slater said. "I scoped it out in daylight. There were no external cameras."

"I guess if we find one, we'll retreat. Besides the painting, what are we looking for?"

"Anything suspicious or out of place." Slater studied the house. "There are some lights on, but I'm pretty sure nobody's there."

"Which door?"

"They use the one off the driveway, behind the Camry."

"Good. It's well-lit, but less visible from the street."

Flipping open his satchel, Slater pulled one of the ball caps low over his eyes, then gave one to Max, along with a pair of black latex gloves. Pulling on a pair himself, next he dug out another purchase from the Russians, the key reader—a thin electronic probe on a length of wire. Plugging it in to his phone, it started the app that had come with it. The screen went black and displayed "готов." Slater didn't know what it meant, but it always started up that way.

"I'll go get the key number and text it to you," Slater said. "That way there's fewer trips back and forth."

Climbing out and leaving the key case on the passenger's seat, Slater slung his satchel up on his shoulder.

Glancing around to make sure he was alone, he walked toward the house, reaching into his bag and flipping on the jammer. It was labeled in Cyrillic too, but it had only one toggle switch, and there was no mistaking when it was turned on, as it displayed a brilliant blue indicator light. That made it hard to forget and leave running, which was important—the device jammed cell signals and Wi-Fi, which was extremely illegal. Most home security systems and cameras worked wirelessly, so disrupting radio frequencies was useful to get past them. Disconnecting the phones and computers of everyone in the immediate vicinity for more than a few minutes, however, would soon draw unwanted attention.

The door at Pilar's driveway had an old-school bell at one side. Slater pressed it, glancing toward the street, and heard it chime faintly inside. Pulling open the screen, he pounded on the inner door with the heel of his fist. Still listening for any movement inside, he took out his phone and slid the probe into the deadbolt. Almost instantly the screen turned green and displayed a lone number: 331.

Grinning, Slater disconnected the probe and texted the number to Max. It was a remarkable piece of tech, even though he had to schlep that heavy library of master keys around, and it only worked with standard hardware-store locks. But most people used standard locks—including Pilar.

Moments later Max walked up the driveway, wordlessly producing the key he'd taken from the binder, from the sleeve labeled 331. Sliding it into the deadbolt, it twisted freely, and Max shoved the door open, head down, the bill of his cap shielding his face. Slater followed him inside and closed the door. They were standing in the kitchen, lit only by the small fixture over the sink.

"No alarm panel here," Max said quietly. "I'll check the other entrance."

Slater followed him into the living room.

"No panel, and no cameras that I can see," Max said, and disappeared down the hall.

Slater adjusted his hat upward, looking around the dark living room. The drapes were closed, so he turned on the lights. The place looked lived in, but not messy, with mismatched furniture, worn carpeting, a big TV set mounted on one wall.

Max called to him, "Come look at this painting."

Slater found him in a bedroom. On the wall beside the bed was an oil painting of Mount San Jacinto, towering over the desert floor. Palm Springs wasn't depicted, but that view, the shape of the peak, was unmistakable, visible from anywhere in that town. Framed in the same simple style as Ty had shown him at the gallery, it could easily be from there, from the California Landscapes exhibition.

"Nice," Slater said, "but it's not the ten-million-dollar valley oak."

Max went back into the hall, and Slater pulled out his camera to photograph the painting. Glancing around the room, he opened the bedroom closet. It was overloaded with clothes, the wooden rail sagging in the middle, the floor below a jumble of shoes.

"Come see this," Max called.

He was in the living room, standing in front of the bookcase that lined the wall opposite the TV.

"See anything odd?" Max said.

Scanning the rows of books, Slater said, "You've got me."

"All the books are new, except these." He tapped on the spines of two gold-embossed leather-bound titles.

Slater saw it now too—they stood out as antiques among the modern paperbacks and dust jackets. Max tipped out one of the books, revealing the pair to be a single object, and not books at all. Pulling on a recessed tab, the side that was painted to look like the edges of the pages detached. It was a container. Inverting it, three fat bundles of cash, bound with multiple blue elastic bands, tumbled into his hand.

"You have a sharp eye," Slater said, taking one of the bundles and flipping through the bills with a latex-clad thumb. They were all rough and used, a jumble of twenties and hundreds.

"There must be twenty-five grand here," Max said, hefting the other bundles.

"Twenty," Slater said. "One of them mentioned this."

Taking the other bundles from Max, he set them on the carpet and photographed them beside the fake books, then stuffed them back inside, replaced the panel cover, and put the box in its place on the shelf.

Max was in the kitchen, looking in cupboards. "Do they have kids?" he asked when Slater came in, moving to open the top of the fridge. "They have a bunch of those super sugary cereals. I haven't seen any other paintings."

"We should go," Slater said. "It's been long enough."

Max closed the freezer, then pulled out his phone and glanced at it. "We've been jamming for four minutes."

Slater went back to the living room to switch off the light, then followed Max out the door. As Max locked the deadbolt, Slater peeled off his gloves and stuffed them in his satchel, flipping off the jammer.

At that moment, a car turned into the driveway, its headlights illuminating the concrete. Heart pounding, Slater kept his head down as they walked to the street, and saw with relief that the vehicle had pulled into the driveway adjacent to Pilar's, across the low hedge. It looked like blue rosemary. The neighbor must have planted that—it was drought-tolerant and well groomed, unlike Pilar's neglected yard full of tree-strangling ivy.

"That was close," Max muttered, once they were at the sidewalk, but he'd spoken too soon.

"Can I help you?" a high reedy voice called to them from behind.

Max kept walking, not looking back, but Slater turned around.

"No thanks," he said, finding a white-haired woman over the hedge in the next driveway, standing beside her vehicle. She had the car door open, ready to jump back in if necessary. Still, it was brave to confront a suspected trespasser out in the open.

"They're not home," the woman said.

"I know," Slater said, casually taking a couple of steps toward her and shifting his cap higher on his head. "Pilar asked me to check on the place."

"Who are you?"

"I'm Josué," Slater said. "Her sister's boyfriend."

"You look a little old for her."

Slater grinned. "Not Norma—I'm with Lupe."

The woman nodded, her expression softening.

"They're lucky to have such an attentive neighbor," Slater said, and waved good-bye as he turned to leave.

As he got into the Challenger, he asked Max, "Did she watch me leave?"

"She went into her house as soon as you turned around. Why did you stop? Now she can ID you."

"I figured I know the homeowner, and I met half her family, so I could spin something. I told her I was the sister's boyfriend."

"I get it," Max said, starting the engine and flicking on the headlights. "That's way better than her calling the cops."

"I know it was risky, but I think she bought it."

"So your painting wasn't there, but what about the cash? You already knew about it. Is it connected to your case?"

"I'm not sure. But you know who bundles up cash like that."

"You think they're drug dealers?" Max said,

turning onto the boulevard.

"I didn't get that vibe. Still, it can't be legit money. If you had that kind of dough, wouldn't you put it in the bank?"

"If it were legit."

Slater looked at him. "How did you know those books were hollow?"

Max chuckled. "I went to a burglar-proofing seminar once. They had hiding places just like that—fake books, fake ice cream boxes for the freezer, a fake box of laundry detergent. 'Junkies aren't going to bother stealing your books or your soap,' the guy said. Working backwards, I knew where to look."

"That's why you were in the freezer."

Slater's phone buzzed in his pocket, and he pulled it out to look. Eli had sent him two texts before this one that he hadn't been alerted to; they must have been sent while the jammer was on. The first one said:

Party over.

And a few minutes later:

Lonesome.

Finally he'd added:

I have a stiffy thinking about you.

Slater thumb-typed a response:

You're not trying to trap me to get me busted for ruining your party?

A moment later the phone rang.

"You didn't ruin the party," Eli said when he picked up. "Barbara deserved that. Everyone thinks she did. Most of them were secretly pleased."

"That wasn't what I was getting when I left," Slater said.

"They're all afraid of her, even the boyfriend. He's an idiot too." Eli chuckled. "I wish I'd seen her go into the pool."

"It was her own doing."

"So, listen," Eli said. "I'm alone."

"I'm not coming back there."

"Can I come to you?"

Slater sighed. "You're not going to like where I live."

"Is it grungy or something? I'm not really a prima donna."

"I read your biography," Slater said. "You grew up in Beverly Hills."

"Sure, but it wasn't all private tutors and skiing in Aspen. I was a black kid in an extremely white town."

"I feel for you, Eli. It must be tough out there on the mean streets of the BH."

Eli sighed impatiently. "So can I come over or not?"

"I won't be there for half an hour or so," Slater

said, and rattled off his address before he hung up.

Max was transitioning onto the 60, checking his side mirror to change lanes. "Got a date?" he asked.

"With the gallery owner. Principal Johnson."

"It's Principal Jackson," Max said. "I didn't know he was gay."

"I'm not sure how out he is."

"Anyway, I'm glad to hear you're keeping your dick out of your cases."

"Shut up," Slater said, irritated. "It's research."

Max laughed. "Shut up? That's all you got? You're getting soft."

Slater knew he was right—knew he was being a hypocrite, knew he risked losing any objectivity he might have had about Eli. He stared out the window at the city flashing by.

As they turned onto the street by the office, Slater said, "I can put all this stuff away, if you just want to drop me off."

"I need my weapon," Max said.

"I'll grab it. Just stop at the curb."

The building was dead quiet when he went in and rode the elevator up to the office. Pulling out the jammer, he plugged it in to recharge and set it in his bottom desk drawer, then opened the safe and heaved the key kit in. Max's weapon was ugly and metallic, poking out of its sweat-stained leather holster. Slater wrapped the straps around the gun to conceal it before he flipped off the lights and locked the door.

At the curb he handed the bundled weapon in through the passenger window to Max, who stuffed it into the glove box.

"Thanks for your help tonight," Slater said, and Max waved cheerfully as he pulled away.

Walking across to the parking lot and his own car, he realized he was still wearing the blue ball cap. It belonged in the office, but no way was he going back upstairs just for that.

———•———

When he pulled into his garage, he reached into the backseat for his jacket, carrying it up the two flights. He hung the ball cap on the back of the door, then spent a minute in the kitchen, wiping the sticky cranberry juice off the black vinyl. It didn't need to be dry-cleaned, he decided, as it didn't smell like booze anymore.

In the bedroom he picked up the dirty clothes from the floor, dumping them in the closet, then changed into a T-shirt. Back in the kitchen he hid the bourbon bottle in the cupboard. As he was scanning the main room, thinking there was nothing he could do to make it look any better, his phone rang.

"I'm downstairs," Eli said. "Can you come and get me?"

"You can buzz me from the front door."

"I'd rather you came down."

Slater wanted to say *I thought you weren't a prima donna*, but instead said "Fine" and ended the call. Stepping over to the grimy window, he saw a black town car double-parked out front, its parking lights on. Not bothering to lock his front door, Slater trotted down to the street. As he stepped up to the car, the rear door swung open.

Eli was wearing the same flattering black athletic shirt he'd had on at the party, and big dark sunglasses, with a little tan bag on a strap over one shoulder.

"What's with the sunglasses?" Slater said. "It's nighttime."

"Can we go inside?" Eli said quietly, closing the car door.

"Sure—just follow the sound of my footsteps."

"They're not that dark," Eli said. "I can see you."

Slater chuckled and led him inside, glancing back as the town car pulled away. When he stepped into the apartment, Eli pulled his sunglasses off, looking around.

"Why do you live here?" Eli demanded.

"It has a great garage."

"It's just so … nasty."

"I warned you about that, princess."

Eli gingerly touched the kitchen counter,

pressing on it, then examined his finger, as if checking for contamination. "Can I see your bedroom?"

Slater led him to it, flipping on the light. Eli stood in the doorway a moment, taking it in, before he spoke.

"I hate to do this, but can we go to the Baltimore? They know me there."

Slater sighed. "You'd better be worth it."

Pulling out his phone, Eli tapped at it and held it up to his ear. "It's Elijah Hardin," he said. "I need a room for the evening. … Thank you."

Slater flipped off the bedroom light.

"Can you drive?" Eli asked him, shoving his phone into his pants.

"I hate parking there," Slater said. "It's such a rip-off."

"I'll pay for it."

"It's not just that. The valets are slow—like DMV-level comatose. The trains are still running. We'll do that."

"You want to take the subway?" Eli said, incredulous.

"Most people who use it call it the metro. The hotel is just two stops. You walk up the stairs and you're right in front of it."

"I don't usually go out in that kind of public place. I'm worried I'll get mobbed by fans."

"How could anyone recognize you behind

those sunglasses?" Slater said, throwing up his hands.

Eli nodded. "That's true."

It wasn't true, Slater knew that. Wearing them around at night would attract more attention than going without.

"You can wear my hat," Slater said, pulling the blue ball cap off the hook on the back of the door. "That way you'll be extra incognito."

"I don't usually wear logos," Eli said dubiously. "I hate to be photographed with them if I'm not being compensated." Even so, he pulled it onto his bald head, then put on his sunglasses. "Can we go?"

Slater grabbed his leather jacket, shrugging it on, and dug in the kitchen junk drawer for an extra metro card. As he was about to walk out, he remembered condoms, and ducked back into the bedroom to grab a few, then shepherded Eli into the hallway and locked the door.

Once they were down on the street, dead quiet at this hour, the storefronts dark and shuttered, Eli seemed nervous, glancing behind them.

"It feels so sketchy here."

"Less so than you'd think," Slater said, and linked arms with him. "I'll protect you if anyone tries to get your autograph."

"Around here I'm more worried about getting murdered. But I believe you could—one of my party guests said you gave Barbara's boyfriend a thorough beat-down."

"Then they don't know what a beat-down is. All I did was dick-punch him."

The metro station was brightly lit, and Slater winced at the transition as they trotted down the stairs.

"Such a large space, and nobody's using it," Eli said.

"Not at this hour. It'll be busy tomorrow morning."

Slater gave him the fare card and showed him how to use it.

"The little gates are so cute," Eli said, walking through. "You could hop right over them if you wanted to." Slater led him down to the platform, and Eli stepped to the edge and leaned over, peering at the tracks below. "Are there rats, like on TV? I've never been on the subway."

"I can tell," Slater said, watching him gawking.

Before long the train pulled in, and when they boarded, there were only a few other people scattered around the car. Slater took a seat near the doors.

"Can I stand, like they do on TV?" Eli asked.

Slater chuckled. "I think that's allowed."

The train lurched forward and Eli lost his balance, grabbing for the pole, grinning like a kid. It was annoying to think the guy had been sheltered from something as basic as public transit, but watching him, the whole clueless thing was actually kind of sweet.

At first Eli rocked with the swaying of the train, but then he lifted his knee and wrapped it around the pole, arching his back and posing with his hand on his hip, like a stripper. Slater folded his arms, watching him, and Eli twirled around the pole. Apart from a couple of wary glances, no one else on board paid attention, but eventually Slater had to laugh. That's all the guy wanted, he realized. As soon as he got a reaction, Eli was on to something else, crouching to peer out the windows.

"Here?" he asked, as the train slowed, pulling into a station.

"It's the next one."

When the doors closed and they started moving again, Eli stuck his tongue out, waggling it at Slater, and then undulating against the pole again, pretended to lick it.

Slater winced. "Don't do that."

By the time they pulled into the next station, Eli was humping the pole. The humor in it had worn off, but watching him gyrate with the elegance of a seasoned dancer, Slater was starting to get turned on.

Rising and watching to make sure Eli was going to follow him, Slater stepped off as the doors slid open, and they went up the stairs to the street.

"You were right," Eli said. "The Baltimore is right here. Who knew."

Walking into the lobby, Eli was in his element now, and pulled off his sunglasses as he stepped up to the counter.

"How are you this evening?" he said to the clerk.

"Mr. Hardin—welcome," the guy said, stepping over and handing him a card key.

Eli took it and flashed him a smile, then turned away, walking toward the elevator lobby.

"That's it?" Slater said.

"They know me here," Eli said, and shrugged.

As soon as they stepped inside the room, Eli pulled Slater close, grabbing his butt.

"I've been waiting for this," Eli said. "You're so damn sexy."

Slater kissed him, running his hands up Eli's back, getting lost in his insistent inviting mouth.

Moving away, Eli sat on the bed and reached for Slater's hand, pulling him down. Slater unbuttoned Eli's fly and grabbed his swollen cock. Eli moaned and slid his hands under Slater's shirt, massaging his chest, then pulled his shirt off over his head.

Slater started to unbuckle his belt, but Eli said, "Let me." Unbuttoning Slater's jeans, he slid his hands inside, slowly pushing them down and exposing Slater's cock. When he took it into his mouth, Slater gasped and closed his eyes, relishing the intensity.

When he got close, he pushed Eli away, then pulled Eli's shirt off, pushing him back on the bed and straddling him. Eli slid his pants off, and they spent a minute exploring each other, Slater marveling at the near perfection of Eli's naked body as he ran his hands over it.

"Are you going to fuck me?" Eli said finally, caressing Slater's cheek.

Finding the condoms and a little packet of lube in the pocket of his jeans, Slater spent a minute massaging a thumb inside Eli before he penetrated him. Moaning at first, Eli leaned into it, deftly countering Slater's thrusts to make it more intense.

"Yeah—fuck me," he shouted, exuberant. "Do it—do it."

It was almost a turnoff, all the yammering, but Slater ignored it, wrapping a hand around Eli's throat as he pounded him, squeezing a little to make him stop talking. After he came, he slumped sideways, collapsing on the bed.

He grabbed Eli's cock, but Eli said, "Blow me?"

Slater obliged, maneuvering between his legs and taking him in his mouth.

"Yeah," Eli shouted, as Slater worked him. "Suck my dick."

It took some concentration not to pull away and laugh at that, but Slater persevered, and soon Eli came, roaring at the top of his lungs, "Yeah!"

Slater flopped on his back, catching his breath, and Eli shifted closer, draping a sweaty arm across his chest. Before long, as he was drifting into sleep, he heard Eli say, "I can feel your heart beating."

———•———

Not sure how much later it was, Slater woke to find Eli out of bed and getting dressed.

"I called a car," Eli said. "Can I drop you at home?"

Slater sat up. "You're not sleeping here?"

"I'll be more comfortable in my own bed."

"That makes it feel a lot sleazier," Slater said, swinging his feet off the bed and rising.

Once he was dressed, he pulled on the ball cap and followed Eli down to the lobby. Pausing only long enough to greet the desk clerk and leave his card key on the counter, Eli led him out to the curb, where a town car was waiting.

Eli climbed in the back, sliding over to make room for Slater, who told the driver his address.

As the car pulled onto the street, Eli rested his hand on top of Slater's on the backseat. Not meeting his eye, Slater watched the dark empty city roll by.

When they came up to the shuttered cell phone store at the bottom of Slater's building, Eli said, "I had fun. It was an adventure."

"Me too," Slater said as he climbed out.

Upstairs, he hung the ball cap on the back of the door, then pulled out the fifth of bourbon and guzzled from the bottle, coughing and sputtering as the heady fumes went up his nose. Wiping his mouth, he poured a tumbler and stretched out on the sofa.

Maybe he could remain objective about Eli. The guy had a great body, so close to perfect that it was annoying, but the sex was odd—loud, and urgent. The golden glow of the intoxicating elixir was percolating into his mind, and he grinned to himself, enjoying the feeling of sinking into it. No, he was in no danger of falling for Eli.

TEN

"*N**o wire hangers!*" Slater woke to the strident voice, trying to figure out what it was. "*What's wire hangers doing in this closet, when I told you no wire hangers ... ever!*" His phone was ringing, he realized, scrabbling for it on the bedside table, and knocking it onto the carpet. Sitting up, he saw his jeans and T-shirt were on the floor. How had he wound up in bed?

"What do you need, Doris?" he answered, once he'd recovered the phone, working to enunciate with his thick dry tongue.

"You're still sleeping," she said.

"Clearly I'm not, or I wouldn't be talking to you," he said, rubbing his forehead.

"I wondered if we're still on for lunch."

"Of course we are. I'm not one of your LA

flakes. You don't have to treat me like I can't keep an appointment."

"You're not nervous that your mother is meeting your boyfriend?"

"He's not my boyfriend," Slater snapped.

"Got it," she said. "I'll see you there."

Setting the phone down, his head throbbed, but not as bad as some days. In the bathroom he looked at the mirror, running a hand through his hair, and spent a minute shaving. If he was meeting Doris, he had to. Before he got dressed he ate the last Pop-Tart, then fished some olives out of the jar, standing over the trash to spit out the pits.

The royal-blue shirt, he decided, digging through his closet, and not just because it was one of the few that were clean.

Backing the Thunderbird into the alley, Slater paused for a minute for a panel truck to rumble past, then after his garage door rolled down, followed it to the end of the block and onto the street. If the truck hadn't slowed him down, he might not have noticed the white BMW right away, nosing into the traffic from the curb behind him.

Slater couldn't remember the plate number he'd written down the other night to compare, but what were the odds that this was a different white Bimmer acting like it was tailing him? Sure enough, when he changed lanes, the Bimmer followed suit.

The best place to deal with this was down-town, and Slater was headed that way anyway. Traffic was sluggish, and the Bimmer kept up with him, never more than a couple of vehicles behind. Once he was in the Historic Core, Slater pulled into the curb lane and signaled to turn into an alley, waiting for a break in the stream of pedestrians on the sidewalk. Platted over a century ago with the rest of the neighborhood, the narrow alley was like a canyon between the backs of the soaring art deco towers.

Pulling in, Slater drove slowly to the other end and stopped a few yards before the cross street. He shifted into park, effectively blocking anyone but a pedestrian from exiting the narrow lane. Halfway along the alley behind him, a ramp came up out of an underground parking garage, guaranteeing a continual stream of vehicles—and there was only one way out.

He'd pulled a similar stunt with the same tail on Friday—would he go for it again? Sure enough, his tail cautiously pulled into the alley behind him and crawled forward, seeming uncertain, but eventually the Bimmer passed the ramp. Now it was just a matter of timing—there were always cars exiting that garage. Slater sighed impatiently, watching the alley in the rearview. Finally a car appeared, pulling up the ramp and into the alley, forced to stop behind the Bimmer. Perfect.

Slater jumped out and strode toward the driver's side of the Bimmer. It backed up a little, and the driver honked, but the vehicle behind honked back—there was nowhere to go. Through the windshield, Slater could see the driver, eyes wide. The guy hadn't expected to get trapped. Slater knew that face, he realized—it was the nosy dipshit Merlo, from Eli's pool party.

"Open up," he demanded, rapping sharply on the driver's side window.

Merlo cranked the window down a couple of inches. "What seems to be the problem?" he said.

"Roll it all the way down, or I'm going to smash it," Slater said firmly.

Merlo hesitated, but the window came down.

"The problem is that you're tailing me," Slater said, "and you're not very good at it."

The car behind Merlo honked, and Slater glanced up to see there was another vehicle behind it now. It honked too.

"I'm on Eli's security team," Merlo said, speaking rapidly. "I just needed to make sure you're not paparazzi."

"Bullshit," Slater said. No way was he a security guy—he looked petrified right now, and knew nothing about stealthy surveillance.

Merlo glanced in his rearview mirror. "You have to move your car."

"What do you want with me?" Slater

demanded.

Merlo took a deep breath and met his eye. "I need to know why you were at Eli's house on Friday. And what was Eli doing at your place?"

Slater had to grin. Finally—that had the ring of truth. "Ask Eli," he said. "Did you put a camera in his bedroom?"

Merlo's eyes grew wider. "I don't know what you're talking about."

"Yeah, you do," Slater said.

Glancing at the cars lined up in the alley, there were three of them now, and they started honking in chorus.

"Stop following me," he said, looking back to Merlo.

"Stay away from Eli," Merlo said.

Slater stepped closer, leaning in and punching him through the window, a sharp left that landed on Merlo's jaw and snapped his head sideways.

"Don't tell me what to do," Slater said, and walked to the front of the Bimmer, pausing long enough to pull out his phone and photograph the plate.

The honking stopped as he climbed into the Thunderbird, and he kept an eye on the rearview on the short drive to his office, but Merlo was smart enough not to tail him any farther. Once he was in the parking lot across from his building, he waited a minute in his car, scanning the traffic, but there was no sign of the white Bimmer.

Once he got upstairs, he found Max at his desk, wearing his dark-red suit.

"You look sharp," Slater said, standing in the doorway to his office. "Are you meeting your client?"

"Later today," Max said. "What's going on? You seem irritated."

"Some dumb-ass tried to tail me this morning. It was the same car that followed me before, the one registered to a dealership," Slater said. Dropping into the chair in front of Max's desk, he told him about trapping Merlo in the narrow alley.

"Do you know the guy's name?" Max said.

"Only what he told me. It could be a nickname, and I don't know how it's spelled."

"What did he say it was?" Max said, turning to his computer.

"Merlo."

Max scoffed. "What's his sister's name—Cabernette?"

"Funny," Slater said, and watched as Max clacked at his keyboard, peering at the screen.

Finally Max twisted the monitor toward him. "Is that the guy?"

"That's totally the guy," Slater said, gazing at the photo of Merlo in a sharp gray suit, a broad smile on his face. "How did you find him?"

"He works for the dealership."

Slater leaned closer. Under the image were the dealership's logo and a name in bold letters: Merlo Gaffney. Behind him in the photo was a parking lot's worth of BMWs, all neatly lined up.

"He said he was a security guard," Slater said, "but I knew that was unlikely. I guess this explains why he's driving the dealership's car. Thanks, man."

In his own office, he sat down and looked up the dealership's website, then read Merlo's bio. Apart from saying he was on the sales staff, it contained only fluff, anchored with meaningless buzzwords like *top-rated specialist* and *customer-centric service*. At least now he knew where to find the guy.

On his phone he checked on Conrad's location. Today he was at work, the green dot on the map at his station. He must have recovered from shaking his ass at that stupid western bar. Dialing his number, he got Conrad's voice mail.

"If you're at work today," Slater told the machine, "could you put your dick away and check into someone for me? I want to know if he's dangerous. I'll send you his name." Hanging up, he thumb-typed a text:

Merlo Gaffney. Age is about 30.

It was time to go, he saw, and got up, stuffing his phone in his pants.

"Good luck with your client," Slater said, pausing in Max's doorway.

"He's not going to be happy, but I'm pretty sure I'll get paid." Max grinned. "Good news, right? We'll make rent."

"You don't have to worry about that for a while," Slater said. "There's a ton of cash in the safe from the Miracle Mile job. We'll use that if we're short."

"I probably won't have to," Max said, "but I do love knowing it's there."

It was easier just to walk to the restaurant rather than drive over there and pay for parking. It was downtown, near Andy's place, less than twenty minutes' walk, which would give him time to clear his head and steel himself for dealing with Doris.

By the time he got there, he was sweating a little from the warmth of the sun. The place was a small Asian-fusion eatery, dark inside, with lots of wood. It was crowded and boisterous with office drones from the nearby Financial District out having lunch. He didn't think he was going to be late, but stepping inside, as his eyes adjusted, he spotted Andy at a table farther in, and across from him was the back of a familiar head.

Walking over, he stooped to kiss Doris hello. Wearing a loose white blouse today, she had a slight build, and these days was letting a bit of gray show in her dark hair.

"My handsome son," she said, beaming at him and squeezing his hand. "You look good in blue."

"How long have you been here?" Slater demanded.

"We just sat down," Doris said.

They both had drinks already, so that wasn't true, Slater thought, and sat between them, picking the side of the table that afforded a view of the front door.

"You didn't tell her that I've got a disability," Andy said.

"I didn't tell her anything about you," Slater said, frowning at him and assessing his outfit. He was wearing a dark dress shirt with a button-down collar.

"It doesn't define you, though, am I right?" Doris said.

"I guess not," Andy said. "But it's important. It's a big … part of who I am."

"It makes me wonder about intimacy," Doris said. "Do you have limitations with that?"

"My god, woman," Slater sputtered.

Andy laughed. "That's such a polite way to … put it. Usually people just … ask me, 'Can you have sex?' I tell them, lube up, and let's see."

Doris cackled, tossing her head back.

Slater glared at Andy and spoke intently. "Stop talking to my mother about sex."

"I like your sense of humor, Andy," Doris said, and to Slater, "I knew you'd be stressed about me meeting your boyfriend."

"He's not my boyfriend," Slater said, raising his voice.

Doris raised her eyebrows. "Of course not," she said innocently, and then shot Andy an exaggerated wink.

Andy chuckled and glanced at Slater. Even with his random twitching, Slater could parse that grin on his face. Was he actually enjoying this?

The waiter stopped at their table, looking harried. "Are we ready?"

After Doris and Andy had ordered, Slater said, "Bring me whatever's vegan."

"How about a noodle bowl with veggie *kamaboko*?"

"Fine," Slater said. "Do you have a bar?"

"Sorry," he said, shrugging apologetically, and was gone.

As Doris gently quizzed Andy about his work, and his family, and his background, Slater bit his tongue, trying to be civil. Eventually he realized there was some value in listening to this—Andy was telling her things that Slater had never heard, would never have asked about.

After their food came, Doris eyed Andy nervously as he started in on his curry and rice. The lack of fine-motor control was alarming, but Andy knew what he was doing, and she had the good sense not to comment on it. Between bites Andy asked Doris about her career and the schools she had taught at.

"What about Slater's father?" Andy said finally, setting down his spoon. "I never got the whole story."

"He was a wonderful man," Doris said. "But I'll leave it to Slater to tell you about him." She gestured with a floret of broccoli caught in her chopsticks and eyed Slater. "Have you been to see your father lately?"

Slater frowned. "He doesn't care what I do, Doris. He's dead."

"But you're not," she said, and ate the broccoli.

Slater had nothing to say to that, and focused on his noodles. After they'd eaten, the busboy cleared their plates.

"So are you a social drinker?" Doris asked Andy. "Slater certainly enjoys his bourbon."

"I'm actually a twelve-stepper," Andy said. "I've been dry for a few years."

Interesting choice of words, Slater thought, eyeing him. *Dry* implied alcohol. Junkies usually talked about getting clean. But alcoholism was definitely more palatable in polite conversation than drug addiction.

"Really?" Doris said, her voice rising an octave, leaning toward Andy. "I'm happy to hear that. Maybe you'll inspire Slater to sobriety."

"I don't need that," Slater said flatly. "I'm doing just fine."

Doris tapped his arm. "Of course, dear."

Slater sighed in frustration. "It's none of your business anyway."

"Except late at night," she said, raising an eyebrow, "when you're on your third chapter."

"He does that to you too?" Andy said. "Slater, you're a drunk-dialing maestro."

"Knock it off," Slater said, glaring at him, feeling his face heating up. To Doris, he added, "Both of you."

Grinning, Doris held her hands up in mock surrender.

The waiter brought the check, and Doris grabbed it, over protest, slipping a credit card into the folder.

"So can I get your number?" Andy asked Doris, pulling out his phone.

"No way," Slater said.

"It's not up to you," Andy said.

"Of course you can," she said, and waggled her fingers for his phone, taking it and entering it for him.

Slater scowled and folded his arms, watching her.

When the waiter brought Doris's card back, they stood up to leave, Andy looping his arms into the cuffs of his crutches. His gait was ungainly, but effective, and he led them out to the sidewalk.

"Where did you park?" Slater asked Doris.

"It was such a beautiful day, I took the metro. I'll either walk up Bunker Hill or back to Union Station." She turned to Andy. "How are you getting home?"

"I live right around the corner, so I'll walk. Or rather, hobble."

Doris grinned. "Funny. Can I walk that far with you?"

"If you can keep up."

"What have I done?" Slater said, half to himself, watching them interact.

Doris grabbed his hands and said, "Bye, sweetie."

"Love you," he said, bending to kiss her.

Andy cocked his head, turning his cheek toward Slater and blinking expectantly.

"Right," Slater said, and kissed him on the mouth, then slapped him on the butt.

Andy yelped at that and laughed as he turned to leave.

Watching them walk off, Slater realized he was breathing hard, but he wasn't sure why. Turning away, he walked back to his office.

Work, he thought. Were Pilar and Jill back from the desert? Pulling out his phone, he paused beside a light pole while he brought up the tracking app. The red SUV was in the Arts District, the circle on the map stationary and within a block of Eli's gallery.

Slater didn't bother going up to his office, instead heading to the parking lot and climbing into his car, then pulling into the traffic and heading to the Arts District. He found a street space a few blocks away and walked to the gallery. On the way he spotted Pilar's wheels, parked across the street. Why didn't she use one of the spaces in the alley?

The gallery was empty, as usual, with Birgit parked at her desk, the rear door propped open. Birgit frowned when he stepped inside.

"You're like a bad penny," she said. "You just keep turning up."

"Such a great customer-service attitude," Slater said, standing in front of her desk with his hands on his hips. "You know, you seemed pretty calm the night the *Hillside Roble* went missing."

"So?" she said, holding his gaze.

"So maybe you knew it was going to disappear."

"Fuck you, cowboy," she said, her lip curling in a sneer. "I wasn't about to freak out and start screaming just because everyone else did."

"You don't care about the art?"

"I love art—I've got a goddamn MFA. But this is just a job. My shitty wages here certainly aren't enough of an incentive to make Eli's emergency into my emergency."

Slater watched her for a moment. "I can understand that. Listen, is Pilar upstairs, or in the back room?"

"How did you know she was here?"

"Just a guess."

Birgit sighed. "I'll call her," she said, and picked up the receiver on her desk phone. After a pause, she said, "There's a client for you."

Slater stepped away, into the gallery. The collection seemed unchanged—the same landscapes hung in the same spots, with the same gaping space for the missing painting. There might be a few more red dots scattered around, so maybe these were actually selling. Soon Pilar came out of her office and stood on the catwalk, looking down at him.

"You're no client," she said, frowning at him.

"We need to talk," Slater called up to her. "Can we go outside?"

"Come up to my office."

Slater shook his head. "No way. Outside," he said, and went to the front door, ignoring Birgit and stepping out onto the sidewalk. Wandering over to one of the carob trees, he assessed the bark, feeling it with his palm. It was healthy, which meant it wasn't being overwatered. At least Eli had hired a decent gardener.

"Birgit's not really a gossip," Pilar said, stepping out behind him.

"It's not about Birgit," he said, turning to face her. "It's about the cameras in there. Do you know a guy named Merlo?"

"Sure—he's a friend of Eli. He was at the opening."

"Does he work for Eli?"

"I think he's more like a boyfriend."

That made sense—Merlo had been tailing him because he was jealous. The security story was bullshit.

"So why was Angela Hayes left off the invite list I was given?" Slater said, watching her.

Pilar's brow furrowed. "I did that. It's nothing sinister. She asked me to keep her name out of it."

"You just do whatever she says? Does she have a stake in the gallery?"

"The gallery is all Eli."

"But she was at the opening," Slater said.

"Angela didn't steal anything."

"How can you know that, unless you know who did steal it?"

"You're looking in the wrong places," she said evenly.

"So why do you have twenty grand in cash hidden on your bookshelves?"

Pilar's eyes grew wide. She hadn't expected that. "Were you in my house?"

"What's the money for?" Slater insisted.

"Who do you think you are?" she said, her face reddening. "Crashing my sister's birthday, and breaking into my house. I'm calling the cops."

"That's your prerogative, but the twenty grand is going to be part of the story. You should call Detective Torres directly—you're already on her radar. Mandatory federal reporting kicks in at ten grand. I'm sure she'll want to see those transaction records."

"You little fuck," she spat. "You won't get away with this."

"I think I already have. What you won't get away with is selling the *Hillside Roble*. Is that all you got for it—twenty grand? You must not be a very good negotiator. Where did you fence it?"

Red and panting now, Pilar hissed, "Get the fuck out of here."

Slater shrugged and walked away, heading back to where he'd parked. It was hard to talk to people when they were in that state. She'd calm down after she went home to check that the cash was still there.

ELEVEN

Once he'd climbed into the Thunderbird, he texted Ty:

Can we meet today?

Before he'd even started the engine, Ty's reply buzzed his phone:

Working. Come by.

The subsequent text had a street address on Sunset Boulevard. Pulling up a map, he saw that it was a coffee place in Hollywood. Slater started the engine and shifted into Drive. Even though traffic would inevitably be slowing down by now, he navigated to the 101 and headed north.

The coffeehouse wasn't far from the free-way, and Slater parked on a side street, walking back to the boulevard. The place was quiet. Even though half the tables and all the lounge chairs were occupied, nobody was talking—most of the clientele were glassy-eyed and slack-jawed, in the thrall of their laptop screens.

Ty was behind the counter with a couple of other staffers. All of them were wearing aprons with the shop's logo on the breast. His name tag, handwritten in big black letters, read TY. When he caught sight of Slater, he cracked a smile.

"It's John Slade," Ty said as Slater approached the counter. "You want something?"

"How about a soy latte?" Digging his wad of cash out of his jeans, Slater set down a fin.

"I'll bring it to you," Ty said, and Slater found an empty table, away from the window.

Soon Ty came over and set down Slater's coffee, then sat across from him.

"You have at least three jobs," Slater said.

"This is a good one. Industry people come in here, so you never know—I might meet the right contact."

Slater sipped at his latte. "That's a realistic approach, at least, considering it doesn't seem like you're getting any help from Eli."

"He lets me work at the gallery," Ty said. "He said he'll introduce me to people when the time is right."

"That sounds like an empty promise to me.

What is it that you want to do in that industry, anyway?"

"I guess what Eli did, and his father too. It's kind of the family business. I thought maybe I could work on a sitcom."

"But it's not happening," Slater said. "Eli's not giving you any connections. You need to find people who can give you what you need."

Ty frowned. "I'm trying to be grateful for what he's done for me so far."

"Gratitude is weakness," Slater said intently. "Eli should help you. If he doesn't, expand your possibilities."

"You sound like my dad," Ty said, and folded his arms. "Except way hotter."

"That's another thing—you should be sleeping with guys your own age. Don't be chasing the OGs. People like me will only use you."

"You're not an OG."

"You know what I mean," Slater said. "Are you working at the massage place because you like the work, or to make money?"

"Mostly for the money."

"Have you asked Eli to help you find something that's better paid, and actually legal?"

"He doesn't know I do that."

"Yeah, he does," Slater said flatly.

Ty scowled at him. "So you just dropped in to unload a bunch of free advice on me?"

"And to ask you some questions," Slater said. "Do you know someone named Angela Hayes?"

"Angela is Eli's ex-wife."

"She was at the exhibition opening. Why is Eli still friendly with his ex?"

"He's a nice guy, isn't he? Plus she used to bankroll him. Maybe she still does."

"What's your sense of her?" Slater said. "Is she a reasonable person?"

"Eli was busy all the time when he was with her, so I don't really know Angela. I wish I did—she's in the biz. A producer."

Slater absently swirled the contents of his cup. "What about a guy named Merlo?"

"Merlo is Eli's current boyfriend," Ty said, "or at least he was. I haven't been up at the house much lately. He's a little prick. Gossipy and petty. He tries to set up barricades around Eli."

"You mean he's jealous of Eli connecting with other guys?"

"Jealous of everyone," Ty said. "Me included. Merlo thinks he's Eli's gatekeeper."

Slater watched him for a moment, then drained his cup and set it down, shifting his chair back.

"Wait a minute," Ty said. "You can't just trash-talk my uncle and walk out. If you don't think he's really helping me, what am I supposed to do?"

"Try to be objective about him," Slater said.

"If you want his help, ask him—don't wait around for it. Maybe call Angela. Use the family connection to set up a meeting. If they can't introduce you to anyone useful, move on."

Ty scoffed. "I have no idea how to do that."

"You'll figure it out. I know you're smart."

"You don't know me," he said evenly.

Slater's eyes narrowed. "Intelligence is a funny thing. Hard to measure, but easy to detect. You're right, I don't know you. But I know you're bright. Take charge of your own destiny." He stood up and walked out to the street.

The kid had a point, he thought, on the way back to his car—it wasn't Slater's place to be serving up advice. What did he know about building a career? Success was any day he made it home without getting shot or thrown in the hoosegow. Climbing into the Thunderbird, he decided to make that stop Doris had mentioned.

His navigation app sent him toward downtown on surface streets. The 101 was more direct, but it must be a parking lot if the software was telling him to avoid it. It took a while, but eventually he was across the river, in East LA. The cemetery was deserted, as it always was, even on Memorial Day and Day of the Dead, when some of them got overrun. Stopping near the familiar plot, Slater climbed out and walked across the grass. Mostly it was yellow and dry and dead, with bare earth starting to show in patches. He scoffed in disgust. Of course there was a perpetual drought on, but how difficult could it be to put some water on this once in a while?

Scanning the headstones, he found it: IBANEZ. Even in this Latin neighborhood they hadn't managed to put the accent marks on the name. He couldn't blame Doris for missing that; she'd had other priorities then—her own grief, and even more burdensome and time-consuming, a crazy thirteen-year-old son.

Dropping onto the hard ground, Slater sat cross-legged, facing the headstone, and thought about the man. Why couldn't he remember the features of his face? There were photos that he'd seen since then. He had to know what he looked like. All he could see was his own surname, etched in stone.

"You were supposed to show me how to do all this," Slater said quietly. "I don't know what the hell I'm doing."

A painful lump had formed in his throat, and he couldn't say any more. Staring at the headstone, he thought about the oblong box, somewhere below him now. He'd only seen it once, the day they'd buried it. No way was he going to get sticky about this. Slater got to his feet and walked away, angrily wiping his eyes. What a pointless freaking reaction that was. What possible evolutionary advantage could there be in having liquid leaking out of your face? Heading for his car, he cleared his throat and tried to pull himself together.

After he climbed in, he took a deep breath and sat there for a minute, willing himself to calm down. The neglected dead grass had given him an idea. Pulling out his phone, he texted Ty:

I need you for an hour tomorrow. Are you working?

His reply came with the predictable alacrity of someone who lived life glued to his phone:

Not until the afternoon. What's up?

Slater texted back:

Keep your morning open. I'll phone then.

Before he could start the engine, his phone buzzed with another text. It was from Andy:

Call me.

A second text from him came right after it, an address with the name of a street that he didn't recognize. He dialed Andy's number.

"I found Angela's home address," Andy said when he picked up. "I sent it in case you need it, but it's in a gated community, so you can't just … show up on her doorstep to harass her."

"I don't harass people," Slater said flatly.

"Yeah, right. I also found out where she's working. This month she's on a project at one of the legacy studios in Hollywood. It's called *Green Blue Green*."

"The studio?"

"The film project."

"What the hell kind of name is that for a movie?" Slater demanded.

"They use code names until they're in post-production and ready to start marketing it. It probably doesn't even have a real name yet."

"Interesting," Slater said. "Thanks for doing the digging."

"So—I love Doris," Andy said.

"You don't need to say that."

"I'm serious. I was expecting a gorgon, but she's great."

"You don't need to be chummy with her," Slater said sharply. "Just … keep your distance."

"Do you want to come by later?" Andy said.

"I can't. Not tonight."

"All right. You know where to find me if you change your mind."

Andy was right, he knew, that it would be easier to get into a production site than into a gated neighborhood. Film people started early, and they knocked off early, so it was too late in the day to look for Angela at the studio. They only worked three or four days a week, but Tuesday was still a good bet as a production day—he'd go tomorrow.

Leaving the cemetery behind, Slater drove back downtown. As he was crossing the First Street bridge, over the rail yards and the concrete drainage channel that was the LA River, his phone rang. Glancing at it, there was no name, but the number had a local area code.

"Ibáñez," Slater answered.

"I met you at Pilar's sister's birthday," a familiar voice said. "I'm not sure if you remember me. My name is Jill."

"Sure I remember," Slater said. "You weren't very happy with me that night. What do you need?"

"I understand that you've been in my house."

"Don't be slinging accusations at me, sister."

"I'm not," she said quickly. "Just—before you do any of your reports and whatnot, I wanted to talk to you. Can we meet?"

"Why isn't Pilar calling me?"

"The money that you found is mine."

"I don't know what you're talking about," Slater said. She could be taping him, or have an accomplice listening in. "But sure, we can meet. Somewhere public. I'm on my way downtown."

"Do you know the Grand Central Market?"

"I may have heard of it," Slater said flatly. "I'll meet you there in twenty minutes. I'll be at the tables on the Hill Street side."

The city glowed in the golden light of the end of the day as he nosed the Thunderbird into the parking structure next door to the market. Inside, he made his way through the aisles, these days mostly expensive trendy prepared food, with a few old-school market stalls with fresh produce still hanging on. Ordering at the vegan ramen counter, he carried the bowl over to a table, and was slurping up noodles when Jill appeared. Wearing jeans and a denim jacket, she had a bag slung over one shoulder, her streaky blond hair pushed behind her ears.

"Sit down," Slater said, through a mouthful of food, gesturing with his chopsticks.

"I don't really want to watch you eat," Jill said, wrinkling her nose.

"That's up to you, toots. You called this meeting."

"I'll be right back." She walked away, heading toward the coffee bar.

Slater was almost finished eating by the time she returned, a steaming paper cup in hand.

"You need to uproot the ivy in your front yard," Slater said, eyeing her as she sat down across from him.

Jill frowned. "What?"

"The English ivy. It's killing your citrus tree."

"I think it looks cool, climbing up the bark."

"If you leave it like that, you're going to have

a dead tree," Slater said intently. "It'll cost a lot more to remove it than to uproot the ivy. That tree is older than you are, and you're its steward. You need to take responsibility and do the right thing."

"I'll mention it to Pilar."

Slater scoffed. "So why am I here?" he said, setting his bowl aside.

Jill shifted in her chair, looking down at the table. "I wanted to explain about that money. You see, I was going to buy a used car. The seller demanded payment in cash, so I took it out of the bank. I was keeping it concealed in the house in case we got burgled when we were out." She met his eye. "Which we did. I was holding it until the seller was ready."

"Bullshit," Slater said.

"It's the truth," Jill insisted, holding his gaze.

"Those bills didn't come from a bank."

"Why are you always so rude? I'm just telling you the facts."

"What kind of car?" Slater said.

Jill sipped her coffee and looked away. "It's a Civic."

"A used Civic for twenty grand? They cost less than that brand-new. Where were you going to buy it?"

"Near my house. We live in Whittier. But you already know that."

"What's the seller's name?"

"OK," she said, and huffed in frustration. "Maybe it wasn't about a used car."

Jill set her cup down and folded her arms, watching him. Slater waited. She'd called him here to convince him not to rat her out, he could see that, but she was a terrible liar.

"I have this relative," she said finally. "He hangs around some rough characters, but he doesn't look rough himself."

"If he's as blond as you, I'm not surprised," Slater said. "It's called white privilege."

She gestured absently. "Anyway, because he looks like an ordinary person, it's easy for him to cross the border. He works as a courier, transporting large sums of money. It's a corporate tax-evasion scheme. But the amounts aren't always tracked. I was in a position to see that—to see that the money wasn't being carefully accounted for. My cousin was preparing for his trip to Mexicali. I took the opportunity and lifted a tiny portion of the total shipment. I'm certain that no one missed it."

Slater threw up his hands. "How difficult was that?"

"Why do you believe that story, but not the car thing?" Jill demanded.

"Because it's the truth."

"How do you know that?"

"Did Pilar take that painting?" he asked, ignoring the question.

"No way." She shook her head. "It was nothing to do with her. We're not thieves."

"Except when you robbed your drug-mule cousin."

Jill's face clouded. "He's not a drug mule. Are you going to tell that to the cops? I'll deny that I even talked to you, and I'll hide that money where no one will ever find it."

Slater scoffed. "I don't give a damn about your income, or where it comes from. I'm still not convinced that Pilar is completely ignorant of what happened to the *Hillside Roble*." He leaned toward her, holding her gaze. "If it turns out you two are in any way connected to that, believe me, I'll come for you."

"OK," Jill said, and took a deep breath, a grin spreading across her face. "That's a relief."

Slater folded his arms and studied her. The threat hadn't intimidated her at all. Pilar kept her passwords under the blotter on her desk, and this one couldn't even keep her mouth shut about stealing from a relative.

"I don't think either one of you are really crooks," Slater said. "I spend a lot of time around con artists and lowlifes, so I know. But I'd advise you not to mess with the drug cartels. Stealing from them is a great way for your cousin to wind up in a shallow grave way out in the Colorado Desert."

"I don't think it's about the cartels," she said, frowning. "It's a company avoiding taxes."

"If he's smurfing money into Mexico, it's definitely about the cartels," Slater said, and rose, walking away, through the market stalls toward the parking structure.

———·———

Dusk was deepening as he drove home, and he flicked on his headlights. Up in his apartment the bourbon bottle caught his eye as soon as he opened the door. Guys first, though. He'd never done it the other way around. It was too risky to get tight and then let some schmuck that he didn't trust into his place.

Dropping into his recliner and stretching out, he opened the hookup app and scrolled through the images of torsos and other body parts. Stopping at a hot guy, dark-skinned and hairy-chested and bald, he scanned his brief description for red flags, and finding none, sent a message:

I want to fuck you. My place. No drugs.

Setting his phone face down on his chest, Slater closed his eyes and rubbed his forehead with the back of his hand. It didn't take long to get a reply from the baldy:

Where you at?

Slater texted him the address and then got up to hide the booze in the kitchen cupboard. In the bedroom he changed into a clean shirt.

Soon there was a knock at his door, and he opened it to find the guy from the hookup app. They didn't always look like their photos, but this one did.

As Slater closed the door behind him, the guy said, "Whoa—what a dump."

"Thank you," Slater said, and stepped close, putting his hands on his neck and kissing him. The guy wrapped his arms around Slater's waist, pulling him close. Even through his clothes Slater could feel the warmth of his body.

Pulling him toward the bedroom, Slater unbuttoned the guy's shirt, and his jeans, then got undressed himself, pulling him down onto the futon, running his fingers over his thick body, grasping his engorged cock. Straddling him, Slater pressed his woody into the guy's belly.

"You said you wanted to fuck me," the guy said, frowning, as if this were a waste of time.

"Sure," Slater said, and leaned over to the bedside table, scrabbling in the drawer for a condom and lube.

Shoving his knees up, it didn't take any work to penetrate the guy, as he was ready for it. Leaning toward him, Slater ran his hands over the guy's smooth bald head, then laced his fingers behind his neck and locked their mouths together, building up the intensity of his thrusts until he was pounding him. The guy twisted his face away, panting hard. Slater kissed his neck and then came, leaning into him.

Once he'd pulled back and caught his breath, Slater said, "Do you want me to blow you?"

"Dude—I already came," he said.

"Seriously?" Slater said, and reached for his dick, finding it sticky and flaccid. "How did I miss that?"

"You were kind of busy."

Slater chuckled and rolled onto his back, covering his eyes with his arm. Baldy got up and went out, followed soon by the sound of water running in the bathroom.

When he came back, the guy said, "I have to go."

That, Slater thought, was very good news. He climbed out of bed and watched him get dressed, then followed him to the door, exchanging an awkward kiss, and locked the deadbolt after he left.

The partly empty fifth was waiting right where he'd left it, and he tipped it to fill a tumbler, then dropped in an ice cube and stretched out in the recliner. There was house music on the radio at this hour, and he turned it up. It seemed to synergize with the liquid gold to slow him down and tune his thoughts to the right speed.

It was so much easier to fuck guys like that, whatever his name was, with no obligations. He had peace right now, no chatting, no pestering, or walking on the beach, or financial planning, or whatever it was that couples were supposed to do. Gulping at his bourbon, he wondered what Andy was doing. Sleeping, probably, sensible fellow that he was. He liked Andy. The guy never demanded fealty, which made him easy to be around. But not tonight. Being alone wasn't always optimal, but decent guys like Andy were probably better off when Slater kept to himself.

TWELVE

It was still early, he saw with relief when he woke, and his head wasn't even pounding. After he'd eaten a spoonful of peanut butter and some stray saltines from the kitchen cupboard, he got dressed and pulled on his boots, then headed down to his garage.

The studio where Andy had said Angela was working was in a crowded part of Hollywood, but Slater found a street space at a meter less than a block away. Walking up on the place, it looked more like an office building than a studio lot.

At the desk in the lobby, Slater set down his business card and said, "I have an appointment with Angela Hayes."

The uniformed guard rose, eyeing Slater, and glanced at his card, then sank into his chair and studied his computer screen, clacking at the keyboard.

"Building 4," he said finally.

"Where's that?" Slater said, surprised it was so easy to get in.

The guard nodded to the doors behind him, opposite the ones to the street. "Fourth building down, on the right side."

Grabbing his card again, Slater walked out the back doors. This looked more like a studio, with windowless hulking buildings lined up as long as a city block, golf carts parked outside the doors. There were people walking around, but nobody seemed to be in a hurry, and the place didn't look busy. Each structure was identified by giant red numbers painted high on the wall. Building 4 had a reception desk like the one he'd just been at, and the reason for the previous ease of ingress became clear—the front-end guard dog was here instead.

A thirtyish woman with heavy eyebrows, she looked up as Slater entered and scowled at him.

"Deliveries are at the side door," she said. "How many times do I have to tell you people?"

"I need to talk to Angela Hayes," Slater said firmly, plunking his card in front of her.

She squinted at it suspiciously, not touching it. "What is this regarding?"

"Ten million dollars."

Raising an eyebrow, she met his gaze, but didn't question him further, instead scooping up the card, stepping out of her little pen, and pushing through a door behind her desk.

A moment later the gatekeeper reappeared in the doorway, followed by Angela. Her hair was still short and functional, the way it had looked in the surveillance video of the exhibit opening, and today she wore tight jeans with a light summery blouse, open at the neck, several delicate gold strands visible beneath it.

Angela gave him the once-over, then said, "Come on back."

Following her in, Slater looked around the space. It was an office, but not hers—it looked temporary, with boxes of files stacked on a credenza, a bare desktop, and on the walls, generic 1930s movie posters in black frames. The only personal item was a laptop, sitting open on the desk. On a table opposite the windows were four big poster boards of black-and-white drawings: even rows of boxes filled with sketches of cars, guns, a soccer ball in flight, human figures running and scuffling with each other, and several explosions, some of it annotated by hand in red ink.

"Is that for *Green Blue Green*?" Slater asked, nodding at the boards.

"Those are confidential," Angela said, stepping behind her desk.

"I'm not in your industry," Slater said, shrugging. "I don't know anyone I could tell them about. They just look like half-finished comic books to me."

Angela scoffed and sat down, waving to the chair in front of her desk. Once Slater was seated, she waggled his business card at him.

"You're trying to recoup the value of Eli's painting," she said.

"The company hasn't paid out on it yet," Slater said, "but I'm looking into it. I know you were at the opening when it went missing."

"Did Elijah tell you I took it?"

"Did you take it?" he demanded.

Angela laughed at that, dropping his card on her desktop.

"Eli didn't actually mention you at all," Slater said.

"I guess that's not surprising. Elijah bought the gallery with my money. Telling people that would be emasculating, so he leaves me out of the story."

"I thought he was successful on his own."

Angela scoffed. "That sitcom was a long time ago. His only significant income in recent years was a big payout when we split up."

"But you're still friendly."

"That doesn't mean I can't be resentful. Elijah doesn't give a damn about art. He just wanted to upgrade his image."

"What do you mean?"

"Look at the big picture." She held up her palms as if framing a scene. "He's an aging actor with nothing to do. The job offers aren't flowing in, and the ennui builds. It was either develop a drug habit, buy a gallery, or buy a vineyard. The gallery was cheaper and a lot less work. It's perfect for him, selling worthless bits of trash for exorbitant prices."

"You helped him find the place?"

"I observed from a distance," Angela said, waving her hand. "Elijah had no connection to the art world. Did he tell you how he got interested in art? He took a framing class. Now he's running a gallery. Have you heard the expression 'too much money for his own good'?"

"What's framing, exactly?" Slater said, wondering if she was talking about something more esoteric than what he'd watched Ty doing.

"It's how you put a frame around a canvas, or a print, or a watercolor. It's a back-room technical process." Her eyes narrowed. "Are you married?"

"I'm not."

"Take my advice—never marry an actor."

Slater glanced at the poster boards. "Your title is producer, correct, for this cartoon movie?"

Angela frowned. "It's not a cartoon."

"Producer means you're funding it."

"More often it means convincing other people to fund it."

"But you have money," Slater said. "Where from?"

"My family."

Slater must have looked dubious, because Angela leaned toward him.

"What, you don't believe that because I'm black?" she demanded. "My father was an engineer. He managed to patent some industrial processes that still pay royalties."

"So you don't really need to steal a painting to support your lifestyle."

Her expression shifted to amusement, and she held his gaze. "I don't—but I wish I'd thought of it. Elijah spent a lot of time on the *Hillside Roble*. He talked about it like it was his child."

"Why did you ask Pilar to redact your name from the invite list?"

"Because I don't know anything about the theft, as I'm sure you've ascertained by now. I don't need to be explaining myself to the police, or to you, or to anyone else about it."

"So you have no idea who might have robbed the gallery?"

"Elijah is his own worst enemy," Angela said. "If he got robbed, it's his own fault. You need to look at his behavior."

Slater rose, and gestured to the poster boards.

"Good luck with *Green Blue Green*. It looks like a real barn burner."

Ignoring the cold stare of the woman on the front desk, he made his way back outside, dodging a golf cart that was cruising by, then walked out to the street. Checking his phone, he found a text from Conrad:

I'm at the station today. Drop by.

Why was he at work so damn early? Such an idiot. No way was he going to run over there on command. Dumb-ass Conrad would have to wait.

Scrolling through his contact list, he found Ty and dialed.

"What is it that you need me for?" Ty said when he answered.

"A field trip. Where are you?"

"My friend's place," he said, and named an intersection in the rough part of East Hollywood.

"I'm nearby," Slater said. "I'll pick you up."

Ty was on the sidewalk a few minutes later as Slater approached, wearing jeans and a T-shirt with his big sunglasses. When he spotted the Thunderbird, he stepped toward the curb.

Climbing in and reaching for the seatbelt, Ty said, "Is this about Eli, or the gallery?"

"It's about you," Slater said, and pulled back into the traffic.

"What about me?" he demanded, staring at Slater. "Where are we going?"

"I could explain it, but I'd rather just show you. It's not far."

"So mysterious," Ty said, and sighed.

"Don't you trust me, Ty?"

"No," he said flatly.

Slater chuckled. "Fair enough."

Traffic was fluid once he got on the freeway, and Ty seemed content riding in silence, looking out the window at the city. On the other side of downtown, Slater exited the 10 and headed toward San Gabriel, soon pulling up at their destination.

"A plant nursery?" Ty said. "What are we doing here?"

"Let's go look," Slater said, climbing out.

Ty followed him into the big yard, walking among the rows of potted trees, shrubs stacked on pallets, bedding plants and herbs arrayed on low tables.

"I don't actually have a garden, if that's why we're here," Ty said, but then stopped, pulling off his sunglasses to look at a dramatic golden bloom, right at eye level atop a potted plant. "Whoa— that's really beautiful."

"It's some kind of chrysanthemum," Slater said, stopping beside him. "I'm not sure which species."

"How would you know that?"

"I studied horticulture in college. In the film industry there's a job for people who work with this stuff. They're called greens keepers, and they manage all the plants used on the sets."

"So that's it," Ty said emphatically, eyeing him, and then gazing around the yard. "You think I could do that, carrying plants around for film production?"

"Not just moving them—you'd have to figure out which ones to use, and go find them, and prune them, and do the repotting. You'd have to learn some things first."

"It sounds like hard work."

"I'm sure it is," Slater said. "But it's a way to get into the business without waiting for a big break, or waiting for Eli. It's a good job—they get paid in Hollywood pesos, like everyone else in the industry."

Ty frowned. "What does that mean?"

"When you're traveling in Mexico, you deduct one or two zeroes from the prices to convert it to dollars. Film industry people get paid like that—take a normal salary, and add one or two zeroes."

"That part sounds nice," Ty said, walking along a table covered with starter pots of chives and brushing his palm along the tops. "But I don't know anything about this stuff."

"You could learn. At least you'd be in the

industry. You'd have a much better chance of meeting someone who could give you an acting job than working at the coffeehouse."

"Industry people come in there every day."

"How many times a day do you talk to anybody about anything besides coffee?"

Ty didn't reply, so Slater gestured toward the back of the yard. "Come and look," he said, and led him toward a row of boxed *Podocarpus*. "People love these because they're lush, and bright green, and they cover whatever's behind them." Walking a little farther, he pointed out a short boxwood. "When these get big enough, you can trim them into shapes—birds, dragons, people. It's a whole art form."

"So you're telling me to become a greens keeper."

"I'm not telling you to do anything," Slater said, frowning. He waved his arm around the yard. "I just wanted you to see how much variety there is with plants. How likely is it that someone will discover you in your coffeehouse? And forget about Spicy Asian Massage. I guarantee no one who comes into that place is ever going to give you an industry job." He sighed. "It's just something to think about."

They went back to the parking lot and climbed in the Thunderbird.

"You can drop me at the train station," Ty

said, adjusting his sunglasses.

Slater started the engine and headed back toward the freeway.

"So do you know anyone who works as a greens keeper?" Ty said.

"Unfortunately not. I know plants, though. They're great to work with."

"Don't they just dry up and die all the time?"

"Not if you know what you're doing. Plants don't mess around—they just exist. No games, no heartbreak, no bullshit."

"Where did you learn about horticulture?"

"Community college," Slater said, and they talked about the field until he exited the freeway near Union Station.

"Why are you so interested in helping me?" Ty said finally, as Slater nosed the Thunderbird to the curb.

"Because you never lied to me," Slater said, shifting into Park. "In my world, that's kind of exceptional. But I'm not sure that looking around a plant nursery will help you very much."

Ty climbed out, pulling down his sunglasses and looking back in at Slater before he closed the door. "Thanks, man."

"Take charge of your own destiny," Slater said, and watched him walk away.

Punk-face Conrad wanted to see him, he remembered, as he pulled away from the curb.

Slater merged onto the freeway, still uncongested at midday, and headed back toward his own neighborhood. Once he'd parked in front of Conrad's station, he texted him, then got out of the car, stretching and strolling up to the front steps.

Stepping out the main entrance, Conrad grinned when he saw Slater. Such a beautiful man—he looked relaxed, and the longer hair looked good on him. Slater admired the fit of his uniform, the cut of his trousers as he walked over.

"I found some info on your friend Merlo," Conrad said, glancing over his shoulder to make sure they were alone. "He was convicted of fraud, but not specifically of theft."

"What kind of fraud?"

"Dude worked at a car dealership in Orange County. He must have cooked the books, because he went away for a couple of years."

"Seriously? He works at a dealership now. Why would another car dealer give him a sales job with a record like that?"

Conrad shrugged. "Maybe he's good at moving product. If it were me, though, I'd keep him away from the money."

"It just seems counterintuitive. There have to be other people who can do sales who weren't in prison for fraud."

"It's about trust, right—there's no risk if he's just talking to customers, but you don't let him use the accounting software. Besides, no one is beyond redemption."

Slater frowned. "That's quite the attitude for a cop."

Conrad laughed, flashing that beautiful smile, and put his hands on his hips. "So tell me about this guy you're seeing."

"I'm not seeing any guy. I told you that. What gossip is Doris spreading about me?"

"She said she met some guy you were dating. I thought that was great news."

"I don't do boyfriends, Conrad. I learned my lesson with you. I vividly remember your jackboot on my head, grinding my face into the asphalt."

"That never happened."

Slater could feel his heart pounding. "It felt like it to me."

Conrad winced. "Well, I hope he treats you right. You deserve to be happy."

Slater scoffed. "I gave up on that pipe dream a long time ago," he said, and walked back toward his car.

Why was the guy so damn infuriating? *You deserve to be happy.* Yeah, well, you deserve a sucker punch. Why hadn't he thought of that sooner, said that to his face?

THIRTEEN

Pulling onto the street, he tried to stop thinking about Conrad. That BMW dealership was on the Westside, near the 405. Navigating to the freeway, he headed west.

Anyone who worked with cars would be all over him about the distinctive Thunderbird, so he parked out of sight on the street and walked back to the dealership. Rows of new Bimmers were meticulously lined up on the lot. Most were black or white, punctuated by the odd red one. The landscaping of the place was deplorable—rolling green lawns and parkways between stretches of new black asphalt, overwatered and chemically treated like a damn golf course.

Walking into the showroom, he was struck with a blast of icy air-conditioning. The only signs of life were a dark-haired woman, sitting behind the counter, who glanced up at him as he entered, and standing beside her, a tall guy in a dark suit with streaks of blond in his hair. He called out a jovial greeting to Slater, then stepped out and approached him.

After he introduced himself, he said, "So what can we do to put you in a luxury German automobile today?" He flashed his brilliant white teeth in a practiced expression.

"I'm Jewish," Slater snapped.

The salesman's smile faded. "So what? You can't beat the precision workmanship of a German car."

Slater put his hands on his hips. "I see you have a repair department next door, though. You can't tell me your Aryan technology doesn't break down just like the Hyundais do."

His brow furrowed, concern in his eyes. "Maybe I'll let you look around," the guy said, and stepped away, back toward the counter.

Slater wandered over to inspect a floor model, shiny black lines with tinted windows. He could feel the eyes of the woman behind the counter fixed on him, but he ignored her. In a place this quiet, his quarry would hear about the abrasive customer soon enough.

He didn't have to wait long before Merlo appeared, his face clouding when he recognized Slater. He stepped around the counter and strode over, speaking in a low voice.

"How did you find me? What are you doing here?"

"I came to ask what you know about the *Hillside Roble*. You were at the opening when it went missing."

"You need to leave," Merlo said intently.

"Make me," Slater said simply, meeting his gaze. "I'd be happy to cause a scene here, if you want. I've got nothing to lose. But I suspect you do. Your job must be tenuous as it is, what with being an ex-con and all."

Anger flashed in Merlo's eyes, and he spoke intently. "I don't know what happened to that painting."

"You didn't see anything suspicious that evening? With your extensive security training, I thought you might have some insight. Was anyone acting strangely?"

"I left that party when Eli started shouting."

"That confirms that you don't really work security for him. No self-respecting guard would run away when things got sticky. Eli certainly doesn't need that kind of help." Slater folded his arms. "What he needs is a gentle touch. You know, to be stroked in just the right way. Those perfect pecs, and those calves."

"You keep your grubby paws off him," Merlo hissed.

Slater chuckled. "I knew that's what it was about. Why didn't you just tell me the truth? I wouldn't have had to smack you around."

Merlo absently touched his jaw. "I ought to flatten you."

"You and what army? That's pure bluster, and you know it. I know you're not packing heat either—if you got caught with a weapon, you'd go right back to eating baloney sandwiches in the big house."

The tall blond walked past, shooting them a curious look.

"I told you I don't know anything," Merlo said quietly. "Can you just leave me alone?"

"Sure," Slater said, nodding. "But if I catch you following me again, I promise I'll beat the shit out of you."

With that, he turned to leave, walking out to the lot and back to his car. Once he'd climbed in, he checked the rearview, but no one was in sight. Pulling out his phone, he dialed Eli, listening to it ring.

"I'm surprised you picked up," Slater said when he answered.

"I saw it was you," Eli said.

"I'm on my way back from the Westside. Can I drop by for a minute? I have a couple of questions."

"Come on over," Eli said. "I'm home."

The navigation app sent him up the 405, and then along the winding hillside boulevard to Sunset Plaza. Once he was in Eli's courtyard, he parked in front of the garage, looping around so the Thunderbird's nose was facing the driveway. Strolling toward the pompous colonnade and the front door, he found it open, and stepped into the foyer. Beyond the French doors, Eli was stretched out on a chaise longue by the pool.

When he stepped outside, Eli rose. He was wearing a tight T-shirt and swim trunks.

"It's good to see you," Eli said, and embraced Slater, pulling him close and kissing his neck.

Slater leaned into him, hands encircling Eli's waist, relishing the feeling of his body.

Eli grabbed his butt and said in his ear, "Let me smoke you."

"I'm not here for that," Slater said.

"Are you in a rush?" he said, pulling back. "It won't take long."

"I'm not just going to whip it out when I'm not sure whether I'm being filmed."

"I took care of that. I told you I would."

"So who planted the camera?"

Eli furrowed his brow. "I'm not going to tell you."

It was probably Merlo, Slater thought, eyeing him, and then sighed. He hadn't come here for sex, but the guy was nigh irresistible.

Nuzzling his neck, Slater said, "Where do you want me?"

Eli cackled. "On the chaise," he said, and pushed him toward it.

As Slater stretched out, Eli sat facing him, leaning in and pushing his knees apart. Slater reached for his belt, but Eli swatted his hand away, unbuckling it and then unbuttoning Slater's jeans. Slater was hard by the time Eli got to it.

As he pulled out Slater's cock, Eli shouted, "Give me some," and then went down on him.

At least he can't verbalize while he's going down, Slater thought, and leaned back, closing his eyes.

Eli was good at this, intuiting the right rhythm, and soon brought Slater to climax. As he came, groaning, Slater grabbed Eli's head. When he pulled back, Eli had a big dumb grin on his face.

"That was so damn hot," Eli said. "You got so hard."

Before he could really get yammering, Slater pulled him close, pressing his mouth to Eli's, hot and wet and funky.

When Eli pulled away, Slater said, "What about you?"

"In movies there's this thing called the sleeper hold," he said.

Slater raised his eyebrows. "It's not just in the movies."

"Do you know how to do it? Guys are always afraid to try it with me."

"I use it all the time."

"I knew it—you kind of had your hands on my neck at the Baltimore." Eli's eyes narrowed. "That's so kinky."

"I mean I use it in my work, not for sex. It's an interview technique."

"That sounds like the hottest interview ever."

"Drop your trunks, and turn around," Slater said, shifting up in the chaise.

Eli rose and kicked off his swimsuit, his cock already engorged. He sat with his back to Slater, who grabbed him under the arms and pulled him closer. With one hand Slater took hold of his cock, and with the other encircled his throat, right under Eli's jaw.

"This isn't how they do it in the movies, but it has the same effect," Slater said. "Just tap me if you want me to stop."

"It's so freaking hot," Eli said, and moaned as Slater squeezed his cock. "You're not going to crush my windpipe or anything, are you?"

"I know what I'm doing," Slater said, and increased the pressure on his neck, reducing the blood flow rather than cutting off his air.

Slater stroked him as he tightened his grip. It must have been what Eli wanted, as Slater could feel him building up to it, his muscles tensing.

When he came, he arched his back, his weight pressing Slater into the chaise.

He released his grip, and they lay that way for a minute, Slater's arms around his torso, his hands resting on Eli's flawless gym-defined abs. Finally Eli got up, flaccid now, and peeled off his T-shirt, then dove into the pool. Slater watched him surface again at the far end, splashing around, then went inside to find a bathroom to clean up. By the time he got back, Eli was toweling off, and stooped to pick up his trunks and step into them.

"Do you want to get in the pool?" Eli asked him.

"I don't."

Eli returned to the chaise longue, casually stretching his shapely legs. "Sit down," he said.

Slater didn't, instead strolling beside the pool to look at the view down the canyon and the hazy distant office towers. "It really is beautiful here," he said, and walked back to face Eli. "So why did you open an art gallery? Why not stick with acting?"

Eli gestured widely. "Actors have long stretches between gigs. It's the nature of the job. We work twelve-hour days for a few weeks, and then there's nothing for months and months. I needed a purpose, something to fill my time."

"Why not open a restaurant, or an upscale bar? At least you'd be around people. All those

California landscapes, the rocks at Los Osos—it's kind of a snooze fest."

"Can you imagine me selling hamburgers?" Eli said, eyeing him. "Besides, that industry has so much competition. The gallery suits me better. That neighborhood is quite fashionable, and unlike food, art is totally subjective. When you walk into a restaurant and look at the menu, you instantly know the social status of the place. With the gallery, I'm the one who gets to tell you what stratum it's at."

"Or Birgit does."

"The buyers show up regardless of whether I'm there or not. I've sold several of those sleep-inducing California landscapes."

"So you're just a salesman?" Slater said, cocking his head. "You don't want to change the world, foster innovative artists, shift artistic paradigms?"

Eli scoffed. "You sound like Birgit. I don't care about all that. I wanted something prestigious to tell people about at parties, and another revenue stream besides my acting craft. Principal Jackson is a cultural icon, but as time goes by, he's losing his cachet."

It was all consistent with what Angela had said, Slater decided, watching him.

"Are you sure you don't want to swim?" Eli said, rising again. "It feels amazing."

"I have to go," Slater said, and went back

through the French doors.

Slater aimed the Thunderbird down out of the hills, riding the brake pedal. Sunset Boulevard was already getting sluggish, and it took a while to get back to his own neighborhood, focusing on the taillights in front of him in the stop-and-go traffic. He shouldn't have had sex with Eli, again. But he wasn't getting drawn into the guy's melodrama, or falling for his con, if that's what it was, so at least he had a degree of objectivity.

Once he'd pulled into his garage and gone upstairs, he eyed the bourbon bottle on the counter. It was close to empty, but that wasn't too worrying; it had an unopened sibling in the cupboard. Still, it didn't fit with his booze rules to get into it now. He needed a clear head. Kicking off his boots, he stretched out on the sofa and loosened his belt to get comfortable, then ran through everything he'd been told in the last few days, trying to winnow the kernels of truth from all the bullshit.

Pilar wasn't a crook, at least not beyond covering up for her chiseler girlfriend. Jill was nothing more than a reckless opportunistic shoplifter. Birgit had an attitude, but that didn't mean she was a lowlife, and the wheelchair seemed like a major impediment to pulling off a stealthy heist. Eli had ridden the metro like a kid on his first trip to an amusement park. But he was also a seasoned actor, so maybe the naïveté, even the overexuberant sex, were all part of an act. Ty's cluelessness seemed more authentic, but he wanted to be an actor too, and any guy who could put on a dress to do sex work had to be competent at compartmentalizing.

Putting his arm over his eyes, Slater worked to visualize it all, intuit the linkages, plan his next angle. Soon he was close to dozing off. Eli had been offended when he'd called the Los Osos painting boring. It was well executed, even if the subject matter wasn't dynamic. The sequoias were better: lifelike but not static. Looking at that painting, he could almost see the trees moving, hear the needles hissing in the breeze. Heavy electrical equipment in the not-quite basement, Ty in drag eating leftovers, bricks of cash hidden in a hollow book. Rogelio with his back to the room. The *Real Meteorologist* tumbling into the water. That distinctive lone *Quercus* on a grassy hillside, worth more money than Max had ever seen.

Slater pulled his arm away, opening his eyes, gazing at the yellowed popcorn stucco of the ceiling above. He had an idea.

FOURTEEN

Getting up, he found his satchel and pulled out his laptop, then sat in the recliner, and using Pilar's credentials, logged into the alarm company's site. Scrolling through the video recordings, he picked one from a few days ago, highlighted it, and clicked on the button labeled DELETE. A message popped up in a white bubble:

Delete video file: This cannot be undone. Continue?

Slater clicked on NO, but it meant that the plan coalescing in his mind would work. Digging around on the website, he found the account settings. Pilar was an administrator, which meant she could create new user accounts—he could create one for himself right here.

In the field for the new user's name, he typed "technical support." Pilar and Eli would still have access to the videos, but now Slater would too, no matter what happened. And unless they dug around in the settings and got suspicious, they wouldn't even know he was here.

Folding the laptop closed, he pulled on his boots and slung his satchel over his shoulder, then grabbed the ball cap from the back of the door and trotted down the stairs to the garage. It was well after dark, and he clicked on his headlights as he waited in the alley to make sure the garage door rolled all the way down.

The parking lot at his office was almost empty, the sewing machines in the building idle and silent as he went upstairs. Flipping on the lights, he went into his office and opened the safe, pulling out the heavy binder full of keys and the lock-reading probe. Stuffing them into his satchel, he locked the safe again and went down to his car, driving over to the Arts District.

Cruising past the gallery, he found it dark, as expected at this hour, the window shades pulled halfway down, with only the dim glow of lights left on in the back. A few blocks farther along was a little brewpub he knew about that had some vegan options, and he stopped in, ordering food at the bar. Even on a Tuesday night, the place was crowded and raucous.

"Do you want a beer with that?" the bartender asked him.

"Just the grub," Slater said.

After he'd eaten, he went back to the Thunderbird, retrieving his satchel from the trunk and pulling on the blue ball cap, shifting it low on his brow. He didn't bother with the latex gloves—he'd spent enough time in the place that his fingerprints would be all over it already. It was a short hike to the gallery, and Slater headed into the alley, walking up on the back entrance.

Glancing around, he made sure the alley was deserted. Birgit had told him the BID worked to keep the homeless west of Alameda, but it must take Herculean effort to stop the tents and overloaded shopping carts from populating such an invitingly dark and secluded space. He connected the probe to his phone and got the "готов" message from the app, then slid it into the deadbolt on the building's heavy crash door. The screen went red and said "ошибка." Feeling the sweat on his neck, Slater adjusted it slightly, rotating it gently and shifting it upward, and finally the app came up with two numbers: 174 and 152.

Crouching on the gritty asphalt, Slater flipped open the key binder and pulled 152 out of its little sleeve. It went in, but it wouldn't budge the deadbolt. Pulling out 174, he took a deep breath and tried it in the lock. It twisted easily, and the bolt snapped open.

Rising, Slater pocketed the key and glanced around the alley again before he heaved the door open, making sure it latched behind him. The hallway was quiet and dark, and only dim light came through the drawn shade inside the glass door to the gallery. Keeping his head down to avoid the gaze of the camera above, he tried the key that had worked on the outer door, but no luck—it wouldn't even slide in. *Of course it wouldn't,* he chided himself—the crash door was shared with the other tenants, so it wouldn't be keyed the same as the gallery.

Looking at the app on his phone, he slid the probe into the lock. This time there was no ambiguity, just one key number: 314. Crouching, Slater found it in the binder and tried it in the door. It twisted freely, unlocking it. He grinned to himself. Every dime he'd paid Igor and Svetlana was worth it when things worked like this.

Folding the binder closed, he disconnected the probe and stuffed both into his satchel, then heaved it over his shoulder. On his phone he spent a few seconds finding the note he'd made with the alarm code he'd seen Birgit use. Once he had it, he pushed open the door. The alarm immediately started its insistent beeping. Not sure how long he had to disarm it, Slater hustled over to the alarm panel by the front door and punched in Birgit's code, then hit the OFF button. The beeping stopped, and the panel's backlit readout said "Ready."

Heaving a sigh of relief, he strode toward the back of the gallery. The place smelled funky, and it was too warm. He could understand why Birgit propped the doors open. Under the catwalk, he went into the room marked PRIVATE, pulling off his ball cap and dropping it on the worktable with his satchel. Stacked against the wall at one side were a dozen or so framed canvases, and he crouched to flip through them. They were all landscapes, and among them he recognized the one he'd watched Ty work on. Maybe these were the works that didn't make the cut for display, or more likely, they didn't fit on the walls but were listed in the exhibition catalog. All of them bore the same sleek minimalist frames that Ty had been building, although they weren't uniform: some had heavy fabric behind the canvas, or cardboard, and one even had particle board as the backing.

Slater carried that painting to the worktable and set it face down, then went over to the wire shelves and found a tray of hand tools among the clutter, scrabbling to find a screwdriver. Ty had used it to attach the frame to a painting, so presumably that's how he could remove it.

A flat box at the end of the table contained frame components—bars and wire and the little clips that held the frames together. Slater pulled one out and examined the mechanism. It had a recessed screw on the side, and the screwdriver Ty had been using fit it perfectly.

Tossing it back in the box, he returned to the painting and used the screwdriver on one of the clips, loosening it, and with a few turns, the clip detached. Soon he had them all off, which rendered the frame loose. Pulling on the corners, it came apart easily into the component metal bars and connectors. The particle-board backing wasn't attached to the painting, leaving the canvas on the table when he lifted it off. That's all the board was, he saw, fingering the edge of the oil painting: a protective layer for the delicate canvas.

Digging through the other paintings in the stack, he considered the likely candidates, but then he stopped, thinking about it, and went back into the gallery. The title card under the sequoias, labeled REDWOODS, didn't have a red dot next to it, but the one marked LOS OSOS did. Red dot: not for sale.

Studying the pair of hooks where the missing painting had been, he saw that the mounting wire would come off them if he pulled it outward first and then lifted it straight up. Grabbing the sides of *Los Osos,* it worked, and he pulled it off the wall. Back in the workroom, setting it face down on the table, he set to work with the screwdriver, loosened

the frame clips and the mounting wire. The painting felt thick, with its cardboard backing, and once
he'd disassembled the frame, he pulled it up. Below
it was the canvas, warm white and marked with
paint smudges and stray brush strokes. Scrawled
in pencil in one corner was a five-digit number in
someone's long-ago handwriting.

But there were two layers of canvas, he saw,
sweeping the frame parts and the wire to the side.
Flipping the back one over, he broke into a broad
smile. It was the *Hillside Roble*. It must have been
here all along—since the night it disappeared—
hidden behind the Los Osos coast. Closing his
eyes for a moment, he tilted his head back, grinning, savoring the rush of victory. He'd been right.

Laying it flat, Slater leaned closer and studied the brushwork. The majestic oak spread its
branches across the sky, the strokes delicate, the
dark-green leaves and the blades of yellowed grass
rendered with precision. Slater couldn't really
see a qualitative difference between this and the
sequoias, or the waterfall at Big Sur, or rocky Los
Osos, but art speculation wasn't his thing.

Pulling out his phone, he photographed the
canvas on the table along with the scattered pieces
of the frame. Turning his back to it, he held his
phone high and positioned the painting in view
behind him, then smiled sweetly and took a selfie. He sent both photos to Della at her Cudahy

Mutual email address, thumb-typing "More soon." She wouldn't see it until morning, and if things went well, this would all be sorted out by then.

Striding back into the gallery, Slater pulled the sequoias off the wall and carried the painting into the workroom, setting it beside the *Hillside Roble* and the dismembered frame. Taking the frame and the mounting wire off the sequoias was quick work, but it took a lot longer to rebuild the frames, the way Ty had done.

First he put the *Hillside Roble* behind the sequoias, smoothing out both canvases to make sure they were flat before setting the cardboard backing on top of them. The frame clips were fiddly, and it took a minute to reattach the mounting wire, but eventually he got it assembled and looking unmolested. Framing the Los Osos canvas went more quickly, and in a few minutes he had it back together.

In the gallery he hung *Los Osos* over its title card, and the sequoias over the REDWOODS label. It wasn't technically wrong to call them redwoods, he thought, assessing the painting to make sure it was hanging straight. But anyone who'd spent any time with trees would definitely call them sequoias.

Once he was satisfied that both paintings looked the way they had before, he went into the back room and reassembled the first painting he'd pulled apart, then set it back among the landscapes stacked on the floor. Slinging on his satchel and pulling the ball cap back on, he killed the lights and went to the rear door, not bothering to lock it, then down the hall, and out the fire door into the alley. He heard it latch behind him, but it didn't matter—he had a key.

Once he'd stowed his satchel in the trunk of the Thunderbird, he went back to the alley and let himself into the gallery again. Pulling out his phone, he checked the time. It wasn't even midnight yet. After he locked the glass door to the back hall, he went to the alarm panel and punched in Birgit's code, then hit the STAY button. It beeped for a minute, and Slater went up the metal staircase at the back of the gallery to Pilar's office, leaving the lights off but propping open the door.

Sitting at Pilar's desk, he woke her computer. The screen was bright in the dark office, and he squinted at it as he logged into the alarm company's website. The recording of him letting himself in the back door didn't reveal his face, he saw, only the brim of the ball cap. It was good to know that tactic worked so effectively. He deleted the file, then the ones that showed him moving around the gallery—turning off the alarm, moving the paintings into the back room, and hanging them again. Once all that evidence was gone, he clicked on the live feed of the camera above Birgit's desk, showing the back door, the stairs, and the door to the workroom, and left it up on the screen.

Leaning back in Pilar's chair, he thought things through. Whoever had hidden the *Hillside Roble* would have done it in the workroom, disassembling both frames, the way he'd just done. If you knew what you were doing, if you'd done it a few times, it wouldn't take long at all. The frame from the missing painting would have become just bars and clips and a length of wire, easy to make disappear by tossing them into the box with all the other components.

Four people worked here, and all of them would know how to take apart those frames. They'd all been at the opening reception. Dozens of other people had been there too, but the guests didn't have unfettered access to the room marked PRIVATE—and it was a stretch to imagine an outsider taking apart those frames to hide the *Hillside Roble,* or knowing that the surveillance cameras wouldn't record anything during a blackout. No, it had to be an inside job.

On his phone, Slater crafted a text:

I know where it is. Meet me at the gallery at opening time tomorrow.

Copying the message, he texted it separately to Eli, Pilar, Birgit, and Ty. That ought to smoke out the rat.

Ty responded almost immediately, a text with three question marks. Slater didn't need to answer that. Reclining, he heaved his boots up on Pilar's desk, and closed his eyes, waiting in the dark, listening to the building, its century-old wooden joints creaking occasionally as they cooled off from the heat of the day. Was it a mistake that he was now the only person who knew where the *Hillside Roble* was? Pulling out his phone, he emailed Max:

> If I disappear before morning, the expensive painting of the tree is hidden in the gallery, behind another painting, the one called *Redwoods*.

Sometime later, he wasn't sure how long, a noise from downstairs roused him from semi-consciousness. Then the alarm started beeping. Sitting up and peering at the computer screen, he saw a figure stepping through the back door. The image was dim, and grainy, and the newcomer was wearing a dark shirt and trousers, but there was no ambiguity—that was Eli. Slater sighed. He wished it had been one of the others. Eli relocked the deadbolt and walked toward the front of the gallery, out of frame, and Slater heard the keystrokes of him disabling the alarm. When he stepped back into view, he headed directly for the painting of Los Osos. Deftly lifting it off the wall, he carried it into the back room. That was all the proof Slater needed.

He waited a minute, then went out of the

office and down the stairs, treading as quietly as he could, and threw open the door to the workroom. Across the table, screwdriver in hand, Eli already had the frame disassembled, the cardboard backing off the canvas. Wearing black pants and a black cotton turtleneck, Eli looked like he was auditioning for a screen role as a cat burglar. The expression on his face when he saw Slater was pure shock.

"Hey, man," Slater said. "Looking for something?"

"Did I leave the door open?" Eli said, quickly recovering his composure. "I'm just working on inventory. I got your text earlier. What were you talking about?"

"Don't even try. I *know*."

Eli's eyes went dead. "Where is it?"

"I've got a better one for you," Slater said, putting his hands on his hips and jutting his chin. "How did you do it?"

A smirk played on his lips, and Eli mimed Slater's body language, sticking his chin out. "It was pretty easy. No one even noticed me taking down my own paintings. I had it hidden and back on the wall inside of three minutes."

"How is that possible? The gallery was full of people. I watched the video."

"Have you heard of the gorilla on the ball court?" Eli said, grinning at him.

"What are you talking about?"

"It's this psychology thing. They show people a video of a basketball game and tell them, 'Keep your eye on the ball.' Halfway through the clip, a guy in a gorilla suit walks through, right among the players. Afterwards the shrink asks, 'Did you see anything unusual?' and most people never did. The players pay no attention to the gorilla, so viewers don't notice it either."

"So the blackout was your basketball game," Slater said, "and you were able to steal your own painting unobserved. You flipped the breaker too?"

"Of course I did. That was part of the plan."

"Did Merlo help you?"

"Why would I give him something to hold over me? He'd use it to bleed me dry. I sent him on an errand while I hid the *Hillside Roble*. He didn't get back until after the screaming started. I didn't need anybody's help."

"Why not just sell the fucker?" Slater demanded.

Eli shrugged. "I had it for over a year, and I put out feelers to the tech people, but I never got a serious offer. I was counting on it appreciating more. Alas, fickle tastes have changed. The robber barons have moved on to the next fad. It was a sinking investment."

"So insurance would pay more than what you could sell it for."

"Exactly."

"If you just wanted a payout, why did you keep it?" Slater asked.

"I couldn't destroy such a beautiful *objet*," Eli said, frowning at him. "Plus I can still sell it. Maybe not for ten million dollars, and maybe not in this country. But there are lots of foreigners who don't have our moral standards."

"Of course," Slater said, nodding thoughtfully. "Why didn't I think of that? Degenerate foreigners. You and I certainly aren't that kind of lowlife."

"Exactly," Eli said, holding his gaze. "It's so easy, Slater. All you have to do is tell your bosses that the painting is definitely gone forever, or it's an insoluble mystery, or whatever it is that they need to hear to sign off on it. I get my money, and then I cut you in."

"That's not going to happen," Slater said.

Eli frowned, pressing his lips into a pout. "But I thought we had a connection. The sex was so hot."

"Totally hot," Slater said, raising his eyebrows. "Absolutely worth waiting for. I won't deny that."

Eli smiled, brilliant and dazzling and disarming, his eyes going soft. It was mesmerizing.

"With you, I feel like a teenager," Eli said gently. "You know that excitement that comes at the start of a romance? I can still feel your fingers on my throat. I really like you, Slater."

"You're so good at this." Slater waved his hand. "I can feel the whole range of emotion. I get why they put you on television."

"You think I'm playing?"

"I don't know—but I can tell you now that I'm not going to be your boyfriend, and I'm not going to help you commit fraud."

Eli sighed, and reached behind his back, pulling an ugly black semiautomatic out of his waistband. It looked like a Glock. He leveled it at Slater.

"Don't point that thing at me," Slater demanded, instinctively showing his hands at his sides. The way Eli was holding the weapon, calm and confident, with his finger on the trigger guard—he knew what he was doing.

"I think your company will still pay out, even if you disappear," Eli said. "You're pretty hot— that was no lie. I feel bad about it, but I'm going to have to ice you. Before I do that, though, I wish you'd tell me where the *Hillside Roble* went."

"It doesn't matter, Eli—you've already blown it. Your boy toy isn't the only one who has access to stealthy surveillance cameras. I set one up right over there, on the junk shelf." Slater nodded to the wire shelving unit at the side of the room.

Eli glanced quickly at the rack, uncertainty in his eyes.

"Mine cost a lot more, though, because I get them custom-built by these Russians in Glendale. Good people—Svetlana and her brother, Igor. Merlo's camera was off-the-shelf consumer junk, but mine streams video wirelessly, right now, as we speak. You know how cloud storage works, right? My business partner, Max, already has my photos of the *Hillside Roble,* and first thing tomorrow when he sits down at his desk, he'll be looking at a video of this conversation. You met him, remember? He was a big fan of *Report to the Principal.*"

"*Report to the Office,*" Eli snapped.

"Right," Slater said. "Max was pissed when I told him how much that painting was worth. 'It's a picture of a damn tree,' he said. I know he'll be glad to hear there's been some depreciation."

"You stupid little fuck," Eli spat, but the muzzle of the weapon never wavered.

From the gallery came the muffled sound of a deadbolt snapping open, and a door opening. Pilar's voice called out, "Hello?"

"We should go talk to her," Slater said.

Eli didn't budge, but he pressed his mouth into a taut line. He was breathing hard, Slater saw, and a vein in his neck throbbed.

"You can't pop me now," Slater said. "That ship has sailed. She's going to come in here no matter what. Let's just go say hello." Slater stepped toward the door, still showing his hands and keeping his eyes on Eli, then slowly reached for the handle, and opened it, and stepped out.

Pilar had turned on the main lights in the gallery. Eyeing the surveillance camera over Birgit's desk, he heaved a sigh of relief. At least now he really was on camera. Even if Eli shot them both, there was still a better chance of someone seeing the video evidence.

"Hey, woman," Slater said cheerfully, stepping toward Pilar, still holding out his hands. He'd never seen her dressed so casually, in jeans and a bulky gray hoodie.

"How did you get in here?" she said, frowning at the sight of him. "And how did you turn off the alarm? I got your text. Were you talking about the painting?"

Eli stepped out behind him, walking into the gallery, again aiming the weapon at Slater.

Her eyebrows shot up at the sight of the gun. "What's going on?"

Slater turned to Eli. "Dude—the jig is up. You tell her, or I will."

"I stumbled on Slater breaking into the gallery," Eli said, and looked to Pilar. "He was acting crazy. You know what he's like. He attacked me, so I had to shoot him."

Pilar frowned. "I'm not going along with that."

"I'll make it worth your while," Eli said.

"No way. You'll have to shoot me too. That'll be a lot harder to explain."

"I'd rather not, of course," Eli said, "but I will."

"Just … slow down." She waved him back with a palm, even though he hadn't moved. To Slater, she said, "You said you know where it is. What did you mean?"

"The *Hillside Roble*," Slater said. "Your boss here had it hidden behind the Los Osos painting, but I moved it. I took photos of it first and sent them to my people."

She looked back to Eli. "Is that why you're waving a gun around? The word is out already. There's no point shooting anybody to cover it up."

"Wait a minute," Eli said, raising his voice, his eyes darting between them.

"Put that thing away," Pilar said. "You're making me nervous."

"She's right, Eli," Slater said. "Even if you ice us both, other people already know what you did."

Eli looked at Pilar, and then at Slater. "Fuck!" he screamed, and lifted the handgun, pressing the muzzle up under his chin.

Slater winced. At that angle, Eli was going to miss his brain completely. He'd survive, but he definitely wouldn't be getting acting jobs anymore—a blown-off jaw wouldn't be very photogenic.

"It's not worth it, Eli," Pilar said, her tone insistent.

Slater sighed, struggling to sound conciliatory rather than impatient. "You made a mistake, Eli. It doesn't have to be the end of the world."

Eli screwed his eyes shut, and gritted his teeth, but his finger never moved from the trigger guard. Finally he lowered the gun, hanging his head, the intensity draining away. Slater stepped toward him and slowly reached for the weapon, dangling now at his side, and pulled it from his fingers.

Pilar sighed audibly.

"Put a bullet in my head," Eli said, not looking at him. "You'll be doing me a favor."

"So much drama," Slater said, scowling at him and stepping away. Popping out the mag, he shoved it in his hip pocket, then checked the chamber, and stuffed the weapon into the back of his belt. Looking at Pilar, he said, "I admire your sangfroid."

She shrugged. "I grew up in East LA. I've seen guns before."

Eli looked smaller now, staring absently at the floor, and his face had gone ashy. Slater walked over and sucker-punched him in the gut. Eli exhaled sharply, bent forward, and stumbled away.

"That's for pointing your gun at me," Slater snapped, following him. As Eli tried to straighten up, Slater caught him with a right hook on the chin. "That's for threatening to kill me."

Eli twisted sideways, lost his balance, and went

down on all fours. Slater kicked him in the ribs.

"Why do you make me do this to you?" Slater shouted, and kicked his shoulder, spinning him onto his back.

Eli slumped flat, immobile now, and Slater held back, watching him for a moment. Stepping closer, he crouched to press his fingers to Eli's neck. His pulse was rapid but steady. Slater rolled him into the recovery position and slid Eli's hand under his cheek.

"Just unconscious?" Pilar asked.

"He'll be fine," Slater said, rising and turning toward her, surprised to see that she had a big grin on her face.

"That was so satisfying to watch," she said. "I've wanted to do that for ages. So how did you figure out that Eli took the painting?"

"After I found it, I sent the same text to everybody who works here. I figured whoever showed up before opening time would be looking to relocate it. Eli took the bait."

"I'm glad I didn't get here first—you would have thought it was me."

"Why did you come in tonight?" Slater asked, his eyes narrowing.

"When I got your text, I wondered if you'd been here during the day. I went on the alarm company's website to check the videos." Pilar grinned. "I thought maybe I'd listen to what you'd said to Birgit, or Eli. But then a bunch of the recordings were missing. I came in to see what was going on."

Slater nodded. "I'm glad you showed up. Your curiosity may have saved my ass." He turned to glance at Eli, still lying motionless. "Can you call the cops?"

"First, maybe I should delete the last few minutes of the surveillance video." She turned and strode over to Birgit's desk, leaning on it and pushing her hair behind her ear, then wiggling the mouse to wake the computer.

"Thanks for thinking of that," Slater said.

She looked up, eyeing him. "Thanks for not making trouble for Jill."

Slater walked back to the sequoias and pulled the painting off the wall, carrying it into the back room and propping the door open. Setting to work with the screwdriver, he detached the mounting wire, took the clips off the frame, and pulled it apart. In the gallery he could hear Pilar on the phone now.

"Yes, *that* E. L. Hardin," she was saying. "He admitted doing it, and he threatened to kill himself. We managed to disarm him...."

Slater pulled out the *Hillside Roble*, carefully laying it face up on the table. It really was just a picture of a tree, but even if it wasn't worth ten million dollars, it deserved to be seen.

Also from Dagmar Miura

That First Heady Burn

The first book in the Slater Ibáñez series sees Slater running surveillance on an injured tech worker and tangling with blackmailers, party girls, late-night hookups with a gamut of guys, and a lot of bourbon.

slater.dagmarmiura.com

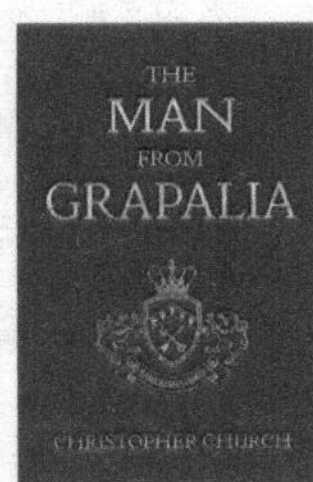

The Mason Braithwaite Paranormal Mystery Series

No one is ever quite sure whether psychic investigator Mason gets results with actual psychic power or his more mundane flatfooting, but the disheveled redhead manages to resolve some intractable mysteries.

mason.dagmarmiura.com

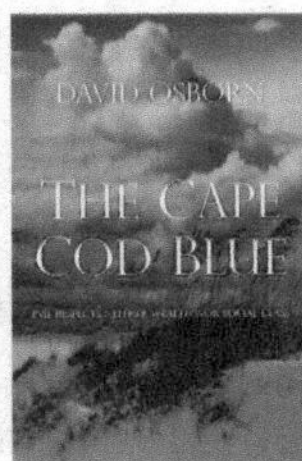

The Cape Cod Blue

The glittering, exalted world of art auctioning hides love, hate, and parricidal murder in a wealthy and socially prominent family when forgery of an anonymous Cape Cod painting is used to steal a world-famous portrait that's worth a fortune.

capecod.dagmarmiura.com

The Bone Bridge

Yarrott Benz, the 2016 Ippy Award winner for memoir, is forced to deal with extraordinary self-sacrifice in this harrowing account of teenage brothers, as different as night and day, trapped together in a dramatic medical dilemma.

bonebridge.dagmarmiura.com